— .✦. —

PRAISE FOR DONNA GRANT'S BEST-SELLING ROMANCE NOVELS

— .✦. —

"Grant's ability to quickly convey complicated
backstory makes this jam-packed love story accessible
even to new or periodic readers."
–*Publishers' Weekly*

"Donna Grant has given the paranormal genre
a burst of fresh air…"
–*San Francisco Book Review*

"The premise is dramatic and heartbreaking; the characters are
colorful and engaging; the romance is spirited and seductive."
–*The Reading Cafe*

"The central romance, fueled by a hostage drama, plays
out in glorious detail against a backdrop of multiple ongoing
issues in the "Dark Kings" books. This seemingly penultimate
installment creates a nice segue to a climactic end."
–*Library Journal*

"…intense romance amid the growing
war between the Dragons and the
Dark Fae is scorching hot."
–*Booklist*

—— .✦. ——

**DON'T MISS THESE OTHER
NOVELS BY *NYT* & *USA TODAY*
BESTSELLING AUTHOR
DONNA GRANT**

—— .✦. ——

CONTEMPORARY PARANORMAL

REAPER SERIES
Dark Alpha's Claim ~ Dark Alpha's Embrace
Dark Alpha's Demand ~ Dark Alpha's Lover
Dark Alpha's Night ~ Dark Alpha's Hunger
Dark Alpha's Awakening ~ Dark Alpha's Redemption
Dark Alpha's Temptation ~ Dark Alpha's Caress
Dark Alpha's Obsession ~ Dark Alpha's Need
Dark Alpha's Silent Night ~ Dark Alpha's Passion
Dark Alpha's Command ~ Dark Alpha's Fury

ELVEN KINGDOMS
Rising Sun
Dark Heart
Storm Wood
Mountain Fire
Burning Sea

THE BASTARD DUOLOGY
The Bastard King
The Uncrowned King

DRAGON KINGS® SERIES

Dragon Revealed ~ Dragon Mine
Dragon Unbound ~ Dragon Eternal
Dragon Lover ~ Dragon Arisen
Dragon Frost ~ Dragon Kiss ~ Dragon Born
Dragon Marked ~ Dragon Forged ~ Dragon Sieged

SKYE DRUIDS SERIES

Iron Ember ~ Shoulder the Skye ~ Heart of Glass
Endless Skye ~ Still of the Night ~ Blood Skye
After Midnight ~ Kiss of Skye

DARK KINGS SERIES

Dark Heat ~ Darkest Flame ~ Fire Rising
Burning Desire ~ Hot Blooded ~ Night's Blaze
Soul Scorched ~ Dragon King ~ Passion Ignites
Smoldering Hunger ~ Smoke and Fire
Dragon Fever ~ Firestorm ~ Blaze ~ Dragon Burn
Constantine: A History, Parts 1-3 ~ Heat ~ Torched
Dragon Night ~ Dragonfire ~ Dragon Claimed
Ignite ~ Fever ~ Dragon Lost ~ Flame ~ Inferno
A Dragon's Tale (Whisky and Wishes: *A Holiday Novella*,
Heart of Gold: *A Valentine's Novella*, and
Of Fire and Flame) ~ My Fiery Valentine
The Dragon King Coloring Book
Dragon King Special Edition
Character Coloring Book: Rhi

DARK WARRIORS SERIES

Midnight's Master ~ Midnight's Lover

Midnight's Seduction ~ Midnight's Warrior

Midnight's Kiss ~ Midnight's Captive

Midnight's Temptation ~ Midnight's Promise

Midnight's Surrender ~ A Warrior for Christmas

CHIASSON SERIES

Wild Fever ~ Wild Dream ~ Wild Need

Wild Flame ~ Wild Rapture

LARUE SERIES

Moon Kissed ~ Moon Thrall

Moon Struck ~ Moon Bound

WICKED TREASURES

Seized by Passion ~ Enticed by Ecstasy ~ Captured by Desire

✦

HISTORICAL PARANORMAL

THE KINDRED SERIES

Everkin ~ Eversong ~ Everwylde

Everbound ~ Evernight ~ Everspell

KINDRED: THE FATED SERIES

Rage ~ Ruin ~ Reign

DARK SWORD SERIES
Dangerous Highlander
Forbidden Highlander ~ Wicked Highlander
Untamed Highlander ~ Shadow Highlander
Darkest Highlander

ROGUES OF SCOTLAND SERIES
The Craving ~ The Hunger
The Tempted ~ The Seduced

THE SHIELDS SERIES
A Dark Guardian ~ A Kind of Magic
A Dark Seduction ~ A Forbidden Temptation ~ A Warrior's Heart
Mystic Trinity (a series connecting novel)

DRUIDS GLEN SERIES
Highland Mist ~ Highland Nights ~ Highland Dawn
Highland Fires ~ Highland Magic
Mystic Trinity (a series connecting novel)

SISTERS OF MAGIC TRILOGY
Shadow Magic ~ Echoes of Magic ~ Dangerous Magic

THE ROYAL CHRONICLES
NOVELLA SERIES
Prince of Desire ~ Prince of Seduction
Prince of Love ~ Prince of Passion
Mystic Trinity
(a series connecting novel)

COWBOY/
CONTEMPORARY

HEART OF TEXAS SERIES
The Christmas Cowboy Hero
Cowboy, Cross My Heart ~ My Favorite Cowboy
A Cowboy Like You ~ Looking for a Cowboy
A Cowboy Kind of Love

✦

MILITARY ROMANCE/ROMANTIC SUSPENSE

SONS OF TEXAS SERIES
The Hero ~ The Protector ~ The Legend
The Defender ~ The Guardian

✦

STAND ALONE BOOKS
That Cowboy of Mine ~ Home for a Cowboy Christmas
Mutual Desire ~ Forever Mine ~ Savage Moon

✦

**Check out Donna Grant's Online Store at
www.DonnaGrant.com/shop
for autographed books, character
themed goodies, and more!**

Dark Alpha's Night

NEW YORK TIMES & USA TODAY BESTSELLING AUTHOR

Donna Grant

DARK ALPHA'S NIGHT
© 2018 by DL Grant, LLC
Cover Design © 2025 by AL June Designs
ISBN 13: 978-1-958353-81-3
Available in ebook, print, and audio.
All rights reserved.

Sneak Peek at DARK ALPHA'S HUNGER
© 2018 by DL Grant, LLC
All rights reserved.

Glimpse at TORCHED
© 2018 by DL Grant, LLC
All rights reserved.

All rights reserved, including the right to reproduce or transmit this book, or a portion thereof, in any form or by any means, electronic or mechanical, without permission in writing from the author. No part of this book may be used to create, feed, or refine artificial intelligence models, for any purpose, without written permission from the author. This book may not be resold or uploaded for distribution to others. Thank you for respecting the hard work of this author.

This is a work of fiction created without use of AI technology (Human Authored™ — Reg #: 6402564, https://authorsguild.org/human). Any names, characters, places or incidents portrayed in this novel are either products of the author's imagination or are used fictitiously. Any resemblance to actual people, places, or events is purely coincidental or fictional.

No AI Training: Without in any way limiting the author's exclusive rights under copyright, any use of this publication to "train" generative artificial intelligence (AI) technologies to generate text is expressly prohibited.

www.DonnaGrant.com
www.MotherofDragonsBooks.com

DARK ALPHA'S NIGHT

THE REAPERS

The seven there are, warriors all.
Do not do wrong or their blade will fall.
Their appearances shrouded.
Their approach, clouded.
Against evil they fight.
Power and magic are their might.
They serve only one.
If you expose their identity – run.
Secrecy is their defense.
If the truth escapes, Death will commence.

CHAPTER

one

Inchmickery, Scotland
Mid-February

The drums of Fate beat boisterously, the rhythm unstoppable.

And unmovable.

It was the first time Daire felt that he and his fellow Reapers might very well lose this senseless war they were embroiled in.

He let his gaze wander around the room, looking at the faces within the confines of the concrete fort their group had taken over on the small isle off the coast of Edinburgh. It wasn't that Daire didn't like Scotland, but he missed Ireland.

There were always seven Reapers. He didn't know why Death chose that number when the group was created, and he never thought to ask. As executioners for Death, it was the Reapers' job to help keep the balance between the Light and Dark Fae.

A job that wasn't easy on a good day.

And they hadn't had a good day in a long, long time.

Death didn't prefer one branch of Fae over the other, which was why the Reapers were comprised of both Dark and Light. Though once a Fae accepted the position of Reaper, they ceased being one or the other—though their coloring remained.

There were two Dark in their ranks—Kyran and Fintan. While Kyran had the red eyes and black and silver hair of a Dark, Fintan's hair and eyes were white. He earned his coloring from killing more Fae than any other in their entire history. But that was another story.

Daire's gaze moved to Talin, who stood with their newest member, Neve, who also happened to be Talin's woman. Next to her was Baylon, who stood with his arms crossed over his chest, a frown marring his face as he spoke.

They'd been deep in discussions for the past hour with nothing to show for it. Daire wondered what the girls, who weren't present, were up to. It was an odd thought. Especially since the Reapers hadn't been allowed to have relationships before.

But all that changed once Bran escaped his prison realm and started his crusade to wipe out the Reapers and kill Death.

That's when Baylon fell in love with Jordyn, Kyran and River got together, and Fintan gave his heart to Catriona. Now, those women—all half-Fae—were making the fort their home. With Death's blessing.

"Daire? Are you listening?"

His head jerked to Cael, the leader of the Reapers. Daire looked into Cael's silver eyes and gave a single nod. "I am."

Daire wasn't as overjoyed as the others to have the girls at the fort. It had nothing to do with Catriona Hayes falling in love with Fintan, and everything to do with the fact that Cat had done what none of the Reapers was able to—wound Bran.

While it felt as if they'd been fighting Bran for eons, it had only been a handful of months, but already, the ex-Reaper had managed to wreak untold havoc.

The worst was during a particularly brutal battle. A clash of magic resulted in Eoghan's disappearance to. . . . Well, that was the problem. They didn't know where their friend and fellow Reaper was, or how to get to him.

To complicate things even further, Bran was somehow syphoning Death's magic, linking the two so that neither of them could find or kill the other.

While it also prevented Bran and his army from eradicating any of the Reapers, the same held true for Bran's men. They couldn't be killed. And frankly, Daire was tired of fighting the same Dark Fae over and over.

"We have to stop whatever Bran is doing," Kyran said, his red eyes flashing in anger.

Daire blew out a breath. "The one weapon we had can no longer be used."

Fintan's white eyes swung to him. "We'll find another. Cat has done enough."

"No one is arguing that point," Talin said.

Neve's lips twisted. "But it would be nice if she could still hurt Bran."

"It wouldn't matter," Cael said. "Bran knows what she can do, and he'll make sure not to get near her."

"Or he could try to kill her," Kyran added.

Fintan's glare grew icy. "That won't happen."

"We need someone or something we can use to kill Bran," Baylon said.

Talin gave a snort. "As if we could find someone who would be able to fight him."

"We don't need to find them," Daire said. "We already know her."

There was a moment of silence as everyone stared at him, trying to figure out who he meant.

Cael gave a shake of his head as he guessed. "You seriously want to ask Rhi to help us? The Light Fae is working her own problems out."

"She's battled Bran before," Neve pointed out.

Kyran grunted in agreement. "Without us asking her. Rhi is one of the best warriors the Light has. She'll do it."

"You're assuming a lot," Fintan pointed out.

Baylon sighed loudly. "This arguing is pointless. Rhi couldn't help us even if she wanted to. Death has had Daire watching her for a long time. Death even wiped Rhi's memories of us—"

"Which didn't work for long," Daire pointed out. "Rhi remembered everything about Death and us."

"There may not have been a formal invitation, but Rhi is part of Death's army," Baylon finished.

Cael sighed heavily, weariness showing briefly. "Baylon's right. When Rhi helped us in the battle that sent Eoghan away, she all but officially joined Death's army. Rhi won't be able to hurt Bran any more than Cat can now."

Daire ran a hand down his face. They'd had one shot. One millisecond in which to end everything. But they hadn't realized Cat could deal a killing blow to Bran until it was too late. Once she was part of Death's army, like the rest of them, she couldn't hurt Bran any more than he could harm her.

It was beyond frustrating. Their options were running out. How could they find someone who was brave enough to stand up to Bran—whose power was growing by the hour—and fight him, knowing they could die? Daire would do it in a heartbeat, but as a Reaper, he and the others didn't have that option.

"So, we find someone else," Neve said.

Talin smiled at his woman, pulling her against him. "It's not quite that easy, sweetheart."

"Perhaps we make it that easy," Fintan stated.

Kyran rocked back on his heels. "Our options are limited."

"There are Fae we can ask," Neve said.

The rest of them were shaking their heads before she finished. Neve was still new and often forgot that if a Fae discovered who the Reapers were, they had to be killed—one of the rules Death put into place to keep the Reapers a secret.

Neve rolled her eyes. "Fine. What about a Halfling."

"Many don't even know they have Fae blood," Baylon said. "Besides, few know how to fight, and even fewer would know how to stand against someone like Bran."

Daire rubbed his eyes with his thumb and forefinger. The Reapers were the most feared Fae of all, and they couldn't kill Bran. But if they didn't do something soon, Bran might just find a way to end Death and send everything into utter chaos.

It was a fekking mess of gargantuan proportions. And he really feared there might not be a way out for them.

He felt someone move closer to him and glanced over to see Cael.

"You look as though you've given up hope," Cael said in a low voice so the others couldn't hear.

Daire dropped his arm. "I've spent the last months veiled while following Rhi. I've learned a great deal about the infamous Fae and her connections to not just the Dragon Kings, but also Ulrik and the Dark."

"You speak of Balladyn."

"Her lover and the new King of the Dark." Daire's stomach turned just thinking about it.

The only thing that made it better was knowing that Rhi and Balladyn were in the midst of an argument and not speaking.

"I've spoken with Con."

Daire jerked his head to look at Cael, reeling from the news. "You spoke with the King of Dragon Kings? When?"

"When Talin appeared on Dreagan land, I knew we'd have to let them know of our existence. Then Rhi told them about us. It was time."

"And?" Daire pushed, needing to know more.

Cael gave a half-hearted shrug. "Con doesn't trust us. Yet. But he'll be a good ally once I prove to him who we are."

"And how are you going to do that?"

"We," Cael corrected him and met his gaze, smiling. "We'll do that. It's going to take all the Reapers."

Daire had to admit, Cael was right, but then again, he usually was. It was one of the many reasons he led them.

"We're going to find Eoghan," Cael stated loudly into the lull in conversation.

All eyes turned his way.

Cael then looked at each of them. "We're going to stop Bran. We are going to win."

"Damn right, we are," Talin said with a nod.

Each of them agreed until only Daire was left. He faced Cael and said, "We won't stop until we've achieved it all."

A small frown formed on Cael's brow. "We'll pick this up shortly."

"What's wrong?" Baylon asked.

Cael turned his gaze to Daire. "Death wishes to talk to Daire and me."

The words barely registered with Daire before Cael put his hand on him and teleported them to a small isle in the middle of a body of water. The sound of distant bagpipes told Daire they were still in Scotland.

"Come," Cael urged.

Daire looked back at Cael to see a Fae doorway. He quickly followed and stepped into another realm, one that took his breath away with its beauty.

Thick foliage surrounded him as the scent of flowers drifted around them. A profusion of melodies from the cornucopia of birds filled the air like a symphony.

His gaze moved upward to see trees towering above them. He spotted some of the brightly colored birds flitting from limb to limb, while others soared upon the currents, weaving between the branches as if dancing.

Daire slowly followed Cael along the narrow path before them —and came upon the flowers. They were everywhere, in every shape, size, and color. Butterflies, bees, and dragonflies flew about, taking no notice of anything but the multitude of flowers laid out before them like a feast.

"Where are we?" Daire whispered.

Cael looked over his shoulder at Daire and grinned. "Death's realm."

If anyone had asked Daire to describe where he pictured Death living, it wasn't this. Then again, he couldn't imagine her anywhere. He'd known she had a realm, but he always thought she just existed in the space around them.

But now that he stood among the flowers while listening to the birds and the hum of bees, he realized this suited her. Death took so much life, but she surrounded herself with other kinds.

Daire's head swiveled from one flower to another as he

continued trailing Cael. It wasn't long before he spotted a tall white tower looming before them. Daire couldn't wait to see what was inside. No sooner had that thought filled his mind than Cael came to a stop.

Daire peered around him to find Death squatting beside a bush with her voluptuous black skirts around her as she fed grass to a rabbit.

"Thank you for coming," Erith said without looking up.

Cael moved to the side so Daire could better see. His gaze landed on a thick curtain of blue-black hair that hid her face. Unsure of why he'd been summoned, Daire remained silent beside Cael, taking everything in.

Finally, Erith stood, the movement of her full skirts making nary a noise. She turned to face them and clasped her hands before her while lavender eyes landed on him.

Daire swallowed. The first time he'd met Death was when she offered him a position as a Reaper. It was rare to see much of her after accepting. That was Cael's job as leader, so Daire was a little apprehensive about why she wanted him there.

He glanced at the black gown that hugged her upper body all the way up to her neck, leaving her arms completely bare. Her beauty was unparalleled, and there were no words to even begin to describe the loveliness of such a being—nor did he presume to try.

"Daire," Erith said. "You've been a great asset to the Reapers. Not once did you complain when I sent you to follow Rhi. You did your duty as I requested, and went even further by protecting Rhi on several occasions."

He began to worry that this was about him talking to Rhi. "You erasing her memories didn't work," he began.

Death held up a hand, silencing him. "I didn't have Cael bring you here to berate you. You were brought here because I wish to know if you want to continue following Rhi, or if you would rather return to your fellow Reapers to fight Bran."

Daire considered each option carefully. "Rhi is special. I know why you wanted her followed. She's stubborn, loyal, at times reckless, but amazingly brave. Rhi has several paths open before her, and it's anyone's guess which one she will take. Her power is . . . fathomless."

"Something the Light Queen doesn't need to know," Cael said.

"Rhi is careful," Daire added.

Erith patiently waited for him to continue.

Daire drew in a deep breath and slowly released it. "I feel as if I can call Rhi a friend. She's still irked with us right now, but that will change. Ever since Eoghan's disappearance, I feel . . . like we're losing. Neve has been an asset we needed."

"Eoghan will always have a place with the Reapers," Death said. "He was one of the first. And he will always be a Reaper."

That alleviated some of the worries that had been bothering Daire. And it made his choice easier. "With Eoghan gone and the threat of Bran increasing, I belong with my brothers and sister."

"Then that is where you shall be." With that, Death turned and walked away.

Daire watched her before looking to Cael. "Now what?"

"We return to Inchmickery."

"To continue tossing around ideas?" he asked, not hiding his irritation.

Cael led the way back through the dense foliage, pushing aside huge leaves as he did. "Actually, I've got a plan."

Excitement burned through Daire when he saw Cael's grin. He stepped through the Fae doorway, leaving Death and her stunning realm behind, ready to get started on this new plan.

CHAPTER
two

Killarney, Ireland

Be ready.

It was a mantra Ettie heard for as long as she could remember. It ran through her head as soon as she woke each morning—and numerous times throughout the day.

She blinked through the fine mist of rain, her gaze on her opponent. Ettie didn't have time to notice the ball of orange rising along the horizon, or how the thick clouds moved swiftly to cover the sun. Or to hear the trickle of the stream running behind her.

The shrill cry of a falcon circling above them barely registered. Her attention was on the direction of the wind as it blew across her cheek, and the way her adversary kept the majority of her weight off her left foot.

Ettie zeroed in on that injury, while in her mind, she planned her attack. When the assault came, she easily sidestepped, leaning back as the wooden staff whooshed near her face.

Spinning, she switched her weapon from her right hand to her left, knocking one of her challenger's legs out from under her.

"Same old move," Jamie said with a curl of her lip. "Is that all you've got, sister?"

Ettie heard the wind before it rushed around them, pulling free long strands of blond hair from Jamie's loose braid and blowing them right into her eyes.

Swinging the staff around until she held it in both hands, Ettie charged her sister. Jamie got her pole up in time. The sound of wood hitting wood was loud in the valley.

There was a clash of strength as each sister fought to get the upper hand—a difficult thing since they were the same height and weight.

Out of the corner of her eye, Ettie saw a boulder about the size of a beach ball sticking up from the earth. She turned Jamie, and vaulted from the rock, which gave her the added height to twist and jab her sister in the side with her staff.

Jamie came at her with teeth bared. The staffs slammed together again and again as Ettie blocked and attacked. She got in a few hits, but just as she tried to get the advantage, the end of Jamie's pole landed a solid hit against her thigh.

"Stop it, you two. You're going to kill each other!"

Ettie and Jamie lowered their sticks, breathing heavily. They eyed each other before turning to Carrie. The youngest of them stood with her arms crossed and a stern expression on her face as the wind whipped the edges of the shawl she had wrapped around her.

"Just one morning I'd like to wake up and not have to come out here to find you two," Carrie said.

Ettie anchored her staff in the ground and leaned against it. "You should be practicing with us."

Carrie's lips pinched. "So help me God, Ettie, if you tell me that we need to 'be ready,' I'm going to scream. We don't even know what we're supposed to be waiting for."

"He trained you, as well," Jamie said.

Carrie turned her ire to Jamie, her big blue eyes flashing. "Another word about training, Father, or 'being ready,' and I'm leaving. For good. I've waited around this desolate place long enough. I want a life!"

Ettie licked her lips as her breathing slowed. This wasn't the first time their youngest sister had said such words. But it was the first time Ettie actually believed them. "You know the stories Papa told us."

"The Fae don't exist." Carrie looked from Ettie to Jamie and back to Ettie. "If they don't exist we can't be part Fae. You two are wasting your lives. Don't you want to experience the world? Find a man? Have sex? Because, I really, really want to have sex."

Jamie barked in laughter as she tossed her staff from one hand to the other before twirling it above her head. She then planted it firmly in the ground. "Are you telling me this is about getting laid? Trust me, it's not worth it."

"Then you're not doing it right. Or the guy isn't."

Ettie wiped her sweaty brow with her sleeve. "Carrie, you're only eighteen. There's still time for that."

"Have you had sex?"

The direct question made Ettie uncomfortable, and the discomfort grew with both of her sisters staring at her. "Yes."

"Oh, God," Carrie cried, her face crumpling. "Even Ettie's had it!"

She didn't take offense to her sister's outburst. Everyone knew that Jamie was the beauty of the three, with Carrie being a close second. Ettie was just fine being labeled not the pretty one because she had other things to worry about.

Like keeping her sisters alive and away from the Fae.

"You want me to find you a guy?" Jamie asked Carrie.

Carrie's gaze sparked with fire. "I can find my own."

"Can you?" Jamie teased.

Ettie gave a shake of her head and started walking to their cottage. "Jamie, don't start. I'm hungry."

Her sisters fell in step on either side of her. Ettie looked around at the surrounding mountains and knew there was no other place on earth that she belonged. It wasn't just family ties that held her to the O'Byrne property. It was the land itself.

Nowhere else on the planet could match the beauty of Ireland and their little slice of Heaven on the outskirts of Killarney.

"Which of you is going to cook when I'm gone?" Carrie asked saucily.

Ettie smiled. She didn't mind the banter and arguing because she knew that one day, both of her sisters would leave the cottage and her behind. Until then, she was going to enjoy each and every second she had with them.

"Not me," Jamie said. "I'd rather be working on an engine."

Carrie gave another roll of her eyes as she flounced into their home, muttering under her breath the entire time.

Perhaps it was because their father had raised them that their hobbies were more along the lines of a man's. Well, except for Carrie.

Ettie walked into the cottage and sat as Carrie placed a plate of food before her. Though Ettie didn't remember much about their mother, she did recall how much she had loved to cook. After she had died giving birth to Carrie, their father attempted to raise all three of them on his own.

That lasted less than a month before he hired a woman to help take care of the house and his girls. Ada had been like a surrogate grandmother who was always in the kitchen cooking up something delicious.

That's where Carrie got her love of cooking, while Ettie and Jamie were with their father. Jamie had a natural affinity for anything mechanical. She could take apart any engine and put it back together again.

As for Ettie . . . nothing came easily for her. She could cook when she had to, and it was passable, but nothing to write home about. But she couldn't fix an engine if her life depended on it.

The one thing she could do was keep the family together. From the time Carrie was born, Ettie had stepped in as mother. It wasn't something she did intentionally, but everyone had a role. That was hers.

She took a deep breath and began to eat. Ignoring the glass of orange juice Carrie set before her every morning, Ettie instead drank the stout coffee that had been her father's favorite.

As Ettie ate, her gaze went to the locked cabinet in the living area. The day her father died, he'd handed her the key to the cabinet, but she'd only opened it once. The night of his funeral, she and her sisters had sat before it and looked through every book, journal, document, and picture within.

Her gaze swung back to Carrie and Jamie. Sitting before her was proof that Fae blood was within them. Her sisters weren't just beautiful. They were stunning. Everywhere they went, heads turned, and mouths dropped open.

"I'm going out tonight," Jamie declared.

Carrie's gaze jerked to her. "I'm going with you."

It was on the tip of Ettie's tongue to tell Carrie no, but she realized that was no longer an option and hadn't been for several months. Her baby sister was of age now and could make her own decisions.

She felt Jamie's gaze on her, but Ettie didn't look her way. She wasn't going to make things easy for Jamie. If Jamie didn't want Carrie to go with her, then she would have to come up with a reason.

"Not this time," Jamie said.

Carrie dropped her fork so that it clattered loudly against her plate. "Fine. I'll go on my own."

"Only if you take a blade," Ettie said.

Carrie began to argue, then quickly changed her mind. "All right."

That was much too easy, but there was no going back now. There was no more talk, each of them lost in their own thoughts as they devoured the delicious breakfast. No doubt Carrie was thinking about the night to come, while Jamie was planning where to take her newest beau.

For Ettie, her thoughts were on things like paying the bills, restocking their food supply, and . . . the Fae. Always the Fae.

Carrie didn't believe, and it didn't matter what proof Ettie put before her, nothing would change her mind. That meant it was up to Ettie and Jamie to watch over their youngest sister. Not something Jamie was exactly a fan of.

All that was pretty easy while Carrie lived at home, but how much longer would that be? For years, Carrie had been putting together a scrapbook of all the places she wanted to visit and live.

Nothing was going to hold Carrie back from her dreams. And Ettie wanted her to get out and live as loudly and carefree as she wanted.

With breakfast finished, Ettie walked from the cottage to the pen to feed the animals. She'd just dumped a pail of food in for the pigs when she turned to find Jamie behind her. Ettie set the bucket aside and grabbed another full of grain for the chickens.

"You have to convince her," Jamie stated.

Ettie sighed as she walked to the chicken pen and tossed the grain to the fowl. "We've been over this a dozen times already. Nothing has changed."

"I'm not canceling my date to watch over her."

"Of course, not. I'll do it."

Jamie gave a snort. "Why do you let her do whatever she wants?"

"I don't. One of us always follows her. Just as I followed you those times you snuck out of the house." She looked over her shoulder to Jamie and raised her brows.

Jamie's mouth fell open in shock. "You knew I did that?"

"Yep." It was by accident, but Jamie didn't need to know that.

Ettie returned the bucket to the others and pushed the wheelbarrow full of hay to the fence where she tossed it to the four horses.

All the while, Jamie followed.

Ettie knew there was something on her sister's mind. She just had to be patient until Jamie was ready to discuss it. Once the horses were fed, Ettie moved to their cow, goats, and sheep.

For the most part, she and her sisters were self-sufficient, but their father had mortgaged the land to finance his travels in his bid to locate the Light Castle. He believed the Light Fae Queen had taken up residence in a castle somewhere in northern Ireland.

He'd died penniless, sick, and without succeeding in his quest. Ettie was just thankful that he'd been at home at the time of his death. Otherwise, they might never have learned what happened to their father.

"What if Carrie's right?" Jamie asked softly.

Ettie patted one of the lambs and straightened to look at her sister. "You're doubting Papa?"

"He said Fae are everywhere in Ireland, yet I've never encountered one."

"Be thankful."

"All these years we've been training to fight them. Why?" Jamie demanded. "If everything in those books inside the house is true, we can't fight them. They have magic."

"Papa said we had to be ready."

"For what? Tell me. For what?"

She shrugged helplessly. She wished she had the right answer, but she didn't. "I don't know."

"Maybe everyone is right," Jamie said. "Maybe Papa was crazy."

Ettie wanted to argue in favor of her father, but the words wouldn't come. Were her sisters right? Had she trained for something that was never to be?

"I just don't want to waste my life like . . .." Jamie's voice died with her words.

Ettie looked at her sister, trying not to feel the hurt that speared her like a blade. "Like me," she finished.

Jamie shrugged and walked away.

CHAPTER

three

Every hour that passed while he did nothing made Daire want to lash out at anyone and anything. He'd opted to remain with his fellow Reapers, but that's when he thought they would be fighting.

"Patience is a virtue," Fintan said.

Daire cut his gaze to him. "Bite me."

"You can't say that," Talin said, cutting him a dark look as he jumped to his feet, leaving the chair he'd been sitting in behind.

"Why not?" Daire asked, confused.

Neve giggled and winked at Talin. "Because I say that to him."

"I think I might be sick." Daire looked at the ceiling.

He was surrounded by couples, and it was . . . depressing. Especially since his mind was on Rhi. He didn't mean to think about her, but the Light Fae was so damn exceptional that it was difficult not to.

"I feel your pain," Cael leaned down to whisper in Daire's ear.

He looked up at his leader, and they shared a grin. As happy as

Daire was for his brethren who had found love, it made him all too aware of the empty side of his bed.

Worse was watching Kyran rub River's growing belly, their whispered words while discussing baby names enough to make Daire want to pull his hair out.

A baby.

Inside a Reaper compound.

He couldn't wrap his head around it, and yet the proof was staring him in the face. Though no one spoke of how things would work with a child. And he certainly wasn't going to mention it.

If Kyran and River weren't worried, who was he to bring something like that to their attention?

With Kyran still rubbing her stomach, River went back to reading whatever book she held. Since she was the only one who could read the ancient Fae texts, they had to wait for her to find something.

"Damned inconvenient," he mumbled.

At least they had the books instead of Bran. There was something important within them that had Bran searching for them, but they had yet to decipher what it was.

Though, to be fair, there were thirty of them to read, and each was well over a thousand pages and almost two-feet long. They were truly tomes in every sense of the word.

"I can't sit here anymore," Daire said and got to his feet.

He had to do something, feel as if he were contributing somehow. Daire strode from the compound and halted once he reached the edge of the isle.

"Is it the fact that you're not with Rhi?"

Daire stiffened at the question. He looked over his shoulder at Baylon. "What are you talking about?"

"Your annoyance, edginess, and all around irritation. Is it because you're not with Rhi?"

"No."

Baylon raised a black brow in question.

Daire turned to face his friend. "Following Rhi was certainly an adventure. She knew I was there almost from day one. She spoke to me, tried to figure out who I was, and allowed me to see the a side of her she usually kept from others."

"And?" Baylon pressed.

"She's amazing. All the stories about her are only a fraction of the Fae she is. But what few realize is that the face she shows to the world hides unimaginable pain beneath."

"For her Dragon King."

Daire nodded slowly. "She'll love him until the day her last breath leaves her. And I believe even beyond that."

"I knew you'd grown close to her."

"As close as I allowed myself."

Baylon's forehead furrowed deeply. "What do you mean?"

"Rhi is more than capable of taking care of herself. Hell, I've seen her glow. I know she could annihilate a realm if she wanted, but there is something about her that makes those who care for her want to protect her."

"It's called loyalty."

Daire shrugged. "It's more than that. Though you're right. I've seen some of the Dragon Kings go to extremes for Rhi. Not to mention the Warrior, Phelan."

"Ah, the Halfling," Baylon said.

"I'm still not sure why Death wanted Rhi followed, but I do know that in the Dragon Kings' war, Rhi is right in the middle of it. Not only because she's friends with the Kings, but because of Balladyn and her connection to him."

"The new King of the Dark," Baylon said and blew out a breath. "There is always upheaval in a transition of power."

"And Balladyn is going to want to show off his might."

"So you believe Rhi could be a key in that war?"

Daire glanced out over the sea. "Without a doubt."

"Maybe that's what Death knew before any of us."

He shrugged, no longer concerned with the why, but wanting to see it all for himself. Now that Rhi had the memories that Death erased back, she knew of the Reapers, but Erith had decided to spare Rhi's life.

That could mean anything in the days to come.

It also gave Daire a chance to continue his friendship with Rhi. He just wished he'd been able to let her know why he wouldn't be following her anymore.

Their heads jerked to the door when Talin threw it open.

Talin looked around until he spotted them. "Get in here, now. River's found something!"

Daire and Baylon rushed back inside the compound to the room that had been designated as the library. Daire skidded to a halt beside Cael as every eye was on River, who stood before a table with one of the large books open before her.

She lifted her eyes and looked at each of them. "I want to preface what I'm about to tell you by saying that this could mean anything. But it's a place to start."

"Seriously, I can't stand this," Jordyn said as she rubbed her hands together and grinned at Baylon. "Just tell us."

Kyran gave River a nod, his red eyes locked on her face. Daire saw the look of love the two exchanged before River looked down at the pages of the book.

She licked her lips. "As we've learned with the books, these were the most important thirty families at one time. I'm not sure why they took it upon themselves to keep such notes about things, but they did. There are cases where many of the families reported the same things in their own points of view. It could be the same with this, but I've not had time to search."

"River," Cael said. "Just tell us."

"Right. Of course. It's just that . . . it's huge," she said, looking at him.

Kyran moved to stand beside her and took her hand. "We wouldn't know any of this without you. Whatever you've found, it's something for us to investigate. Sweetheart, we can't do that unless you tell us."

River's pale blue gaze returned to Cael. "Do you know if Bran ever sired a child?"

Everyone turned their eyes to Cael.

He slowly shook his head. "He didn't speak of his time before he was a Reaper. Anything is possible, why?"

"This book, this family mentions Ó Broin."

"The descendant of Bran," Daire said.

Cat's eyes bulged. "I know this. It's an Irish legend about a mariner named Bran who went on many adventures. His name means raven in Irish."

"This can't be some quirk of chance," Kyran said.

Neve fingered the hilt of one of her many knives. "It looks like we need to discover if there are indeed descendants of Bran."

"The Anglicized name is O'Byrne," River replied.

Cael smiled at River. "Good work. I'll talk to Erith. She would know if Bran had any children."

"Bloody hell," Talin said as he ran a hand through his black hair after Cael teleported away.

Daire made his way to River. "Can you get me dates of when the name would've changed to O'Byrne?"

"I sure can."

Cat and Jordyn walked to them. Cat then said, "You want a list of everyone with that name?"

"I do," Daire said with a nod.

Cat smiled and held out her hand as she used her magic. In seconds, there was a huge stack of papers that she handed to him. Daire took them, flipping through to see that it was indeed a list of everyone with that name, their age, and where they lived.

"Damn, girl," Jordyn said with a grin. "I'm loving having you around."

River nodded to the papers. "That's going to take some time to get through."

Jordyn then turned to Cat. "I don't suppose you could just wish the people here?"

"No," Fintan said as he came up behind Cat. "She's not ready for something of that magnitude yet."

"It's fine," Daire said while perusing the pages when Cat started to argue. "You also put them in order of family. Thanks." He raised his gaze to her. "It's going to take some work, but we can do this."

Cat held out her hand again. Another large stack appeared. "You're going to need every listing of the Ó Broin, as well."

"That won't go back nearly far enough," Kyran said.

Baylon ran his thumb along the edges of one stack. "And these are only mortals. We'll need Fae records, as well."

"We'll get that," Neve said as she looked at Kyran.

And then they were gone.

When the others began discussing how to trace the line through generations when the humans didn't keep records, Daire took the two piles of papers and found an empty room.

He started with the most recent family and began to trace the line as far back as he could. Then he moved on to the next family, and the next, and the next.

Using the walls, he gave each family a section and different colored thread and worked his way down the line until he could go no more. He didn't know how long he worked. He'd found something he could focus on, and he dove right into it.

After he'd completed each of the families from the mortal stacks, he began on the Fae after Neve and Talin returned with the files. He was halfway through the Fae when Cael and Fintan walked into the room.

"Damn," Fintan murmured.

Daire stood back and looked around the room. He hadn't remembered using the ceiling and floor, but then again, he'd been utterly engrossed in his task.

He turned to Cael. "Do you have news?"

"It seems Bran left five children behind," Cael announced.

Daire had known it would be difficult finding one, but five? Their task just got that much harder. "Do the others know?"

"They do," Fintan said.

Cael walked into the room and looked around as he spoke. "Three of Bran's children were Fae. Two were Halflings."

"We have to trace each of those five children," Daire said.

Fintan made a sound at the back of his throat. "This gives me a headache. Find me someone to kill, and I'll do it. But I'm useless in this."

Daire waited until Fintan was gone before he turned to Cael. "Five?"

"Five. We don't speak of our pasts, so why would we talk of children?"

It was true, but still. Daire narrowed his gaze on Cael. "Do you have any?"

"Kids?" Cael asked and then promptly shook his head. "Not that I know of."

"Me either."

And it was something Daire was thankful for. He wasn't sure he could keep from checking on them if he did. Not even being a Reaper would prevent that.

"Bran left his wife and three kids behind when he became a Reaper," Cael said.

Daire frowned. "I left no one behind, so it was easy for me to choose to be a Reaper. How did he do it?"

"I don't know. Maybe that's why it was hard for him to be alone."

Though it was an unspoken decree that they not ask each other about their pasts, Daire couldn't help himself. "Did you leave anyone behind?"

"Yes," Cael said, his gaze going distant. Then he seemed to mentally shake himself. "We've got work to do. There are descendants of Bran out there, and we need to find them."

"You really think they can help us?"

"I'd rather they be on our side than his."

Damn. Daire hadn't even thought of that.

CHAPTER

four

The available men lacked in . . . well, everything. Ettie's head throbbed from the loud noise of the pub. She craved fresh air from the press of bodies and the odor of someone that made her gag.

How in the world did her sisters find taverns even remotely entertaining? Ettie had long ago stopped trying to figure her siblings out. They were vastly different than her, and she accepted that.

Though it made her feel isolated and incredibly . . . lonely. She would never tell them that, though. They had enough on their plates to deal with. This was her burden.

She looked through the crowd to find Carrie. Her youngest sister wore a thin, soft pink sweater that made her skin look as if it glowed. As soon as Carrie planted her jean-clad butt on a bar stool, man after man flocked to her. Carrie had yet to pay for a drink after almost two hours at the pub.

At least Ettie wouldn't have to worry about her youngest sister not finding happiness. Carrie was a free spirit who liked to follow rainbows. She didn't see the gritty, ugly world as it truly was. No, Carrie only saw possibilities and hope.

And who was Ettie to crush that?

She turned her head to look out the window and spotted Jamie holding hands with her new beau as she gave him a dazzling smile. None of the men who dated Jamie seemed to mind that she loved engines and grease. They only cared about her.

Ettie sat back and watched until Jamie and her man disappeared from view. So many nights, she'd silently griped to herself about chasing her siblings around to make sure they were safe, but now, knowing that their time with her was about to end, she longed for them to remain.

"Am I interrupting?"

She jerked her head up at the sound of the deep voice to find a man standing at her table. He had a nice smile, silver eyes, and thick, gorgeous black hair that was pulled back at the base of his neck. "Do you need a chair?" she asked.

His smile widened. "Aye. I suppose I do. But to sit with you."

Ettie was so shocked that she blinked up at him. No one ever wanted to sit with her. "Ah . . . sure."

"You seem surprised," he said as he lowered himself into the chair and set down his ale.

She shrugged, unsure how to respond.

"Would you like another ale?" he asked.

Usually, her limit was one, but she wasn't going to pass up the opportunity to have someone buy her a drink. "That would be nice."

She couldn't take her eyes off him as he stood and waved to the bartender. The man was tall, wide-shouldered, and had a voice as smooth as velvet. And he was gorgeous.

Stunningly so.

It made her nervous to have such a man pay attention to her. When he sat back down and turned those eyes of his to her, she lost her train of thought.

"Why is a woman like you sitting alone?" he asked with a grin.

Her ale was passed from the bartender through the crowd to her. She accepted it and took a long drink, hoping it would calm her nerves.

It didn't.

She wasn't going to tell him she was there to watch over her sister. God. That would make him realize just what a loser she really was.

"Are you new in town?" She hoped to change the subject, but she also wanted to know more about him.

A man who looked as delicious as he did would be whispered about all over town. And Ettie had heard nothing. Neither had her sisters because they would've been all over him.

Just then, Carrie's gaze landed on the stranger. Her eyes widened when she saw his face, but she couldn't extract herself from her gaggle of men. And for once, Ettie was thankful.

"I am new," the man said. "Is it obvious?"

Ettie found herself smiling. "A man who looks like you can't come here and not cause a ruckus."

"Do you like what you see, then?"

She laughed and relaxed as their banter continued. "You're very confident, which means you have no trouble getting any woman you want. That leads me to believe that you know exactly how handsome you are."

"I just want to know if you think I'm handsome."

"I do."

His lips curved into a smile. "Good. Because I think you're beautiful."

Now she knew something was wrong with him. His interest would change as soon as he got a look at Jamie or Carrie, but Ettie was going to bask in his attention for now.

She stuck out her hand, "I'm Et—"

"No names," he said over her.

Frowning, she lowered her hand, suddenly wary. "Why?"

"Let's get to know each other differently. Everyone introduces themselves with their names first. People then make assumptions on those names."

"I suppose."

"You know I'm right."

"So, you want to talk without knowing my name?"

He gave a nod and crossed an ankle over his knee. "Up for the challenge?"

Ettie watched him for a moment. Why couldn't she have some fun? Her sisters didn't think twice about it. And she knew what to look for in a Fae, so she'd be more careful than either Jamie or Carrie.

"Sure."

"I knew you wouldn't let me down," he said with a wink as he brought his glass to his lips and held her gaze as he drank.

Feeling more carefree than she had in years, Ettie sipped more ale. "What brings you to Killarney?"

"I've been traveling all over Ireland and even a bit of Scotland," he replied.

"How interesting." She hadn't been outside of Killarney, and she was dying to experience more of the world than just through pictures. "Where is your favorite part?"

"I'd have to say right here."

Ettie knew he was flirting. And it felt wonderful! She returned his smile, intending to play along. "Our countryside is quite beautiful."

"I was referring to you."

She felt her cheeks heat. No wonder Jamie always had a boyfriend, and Carrie was dying to date. This attention and, yes, even the attraction, gave Ettie's confidence a boost she hadn't realized was lacking.

He put his forearms on the table and leaned toward her. "If I'd known a compliment would make you blush, it would've been the first thing I did."

"Hey," Carrie said as she walked up.

The smile died on Ettie's lips. Whatever fun she'd been having would be dashed after her visitor got a look at Carrie's beautiful face. "Hi."

"Who's this?" Carrie said as her gaze moved to the man.

He gave Carrie a nod, but to Ettie's surprise, his gaze returned to her.

"I'm a new friend," he replied.

Carrie snorted. "Ettie doesn't have friends."

Not only had her sister embarrassed her, but she'd also given her name. Anger bubbled within Ettie. She stood and put her back to the man as she leaned close to Carrie.

"Really?" Ettie said through clenched teeth. "I don't bother you. Do you have to have every fekking man around sniffing at you? Can't I have one hour of fun?"

Carrie jerked back, fury contorting her face. "What the hell is wrong with you? I was just coming to say hello."

"No. You were flirting. It's not enough that you have every single man—and even the married ones—staring at you. You had to come over and see who wasn't paying you homage."

"Get over yourself," Carrie said angrily and spun away.

For a long minute, Ettie remained where she was. It wasn't like her to lose her temper like that, but she wouldn't apologize.

"Let's go for a walk."

She hadn't even heard the man stand, much less come up behind her. Ettie turned to him and looked up into his silver eyes. "I can't go far."

"We won't. I promise."

Without a backward glance at Carrie, Ettie walked out of the pub, grabbing her coat on the way. As soon as they exited the building, she drank in the quiet. She lifted her face to the sky and took a deep breath as the cool air brushed against her cheek.

She shrugged into her jacket and looked at the man with his wide shoulders and stunning smile. "You know my name now."

"I do. It seems only fair that you know mine."

They began to walk slowly along the sidewalk. "It does."

"I'm Bran."

"It's nice to meet you, Bran," she said as they grinned at each other.

His smile was a heart-skipping combination of charming and sexy. "It's very nice to know you, Ettie."

He walked with her with nothing more on for warmth than his thick, cream sweater. Ettie ignored Jamie, who stopped in her tracks when she spotted them from across the street.

"You're being stared at," he leaned close to whisper.

She threw Jamie a look. "Gawked at, actually. That's my sister."

"Ah. I see. And the young lady in the pub?"

"My youngest sister."

He gave a nod of his black head. "They're protective."

She wasn't going to make things awkward by telling him he was wrong. Let him believe what he would. It wasn't as if she'd see more of him. Bran was a wanderer, and it wouldn't be long before he left.

"Do you have siblings?" she asked.

He briefly met her gaze. "Sadly, no. I bet it's nice to have such family."

"Well, it depends on who you ask and what day you do the asking."

Bran laughed, their gazes meeting. He stopped and faced her. "I wish I'd traveled to Killarney much sooner. You're a delight I hadn't anticipated."

"Do you always know what to say?"

"Hardly," he said with crooked smile.

Her brow rose. "I doubt that."

"Why do you say that?"

She shrugged and put her hands in her coat pockets. "It's that confidence I spoke of earlier."

"The same kind you have, you mean?"

That made her laugh out loud. "If you only knew the truth."

"Tell me," he urged.

She widened her eyes while shaking her head. "I think I'd rather you believe the fiction."

"All right. How about I tell you something about me first."

The dare was out there, and she found she didn't want to let it pass her by. "I accept."

"I've not had a woman catch my eye in . . . some time. Then I saw you."

She was drowning in his eyes. Even when he stepped closer, she didn't back away. When was the last time a man who was interested in her was this close? She craved the attention, hungered for it.

Like she needed air to breathe.

"I was at the pub to watch over Carrie. Once people see my sisters, I'm forgotten."

He closed the distance between them and lightly skimmed his fingers along her cheek to her jaw. "I only saw you."

"Yes, you did."

Her eyes slid closed as his head lowered to hers. Just as his lips were about to touch hers, someone cleared their throat right beside her.

Ettie jerked back and looked to find Jamie standing with her arms crossed over her chest and her lips pinched. Beside her was Carrie with a murderous expression on her face.

"Can I help you?" she asked her sisters.

Bran pulled her hand from her pocket and kissed her knuckles. "I'll see you soon, Ettie."

She watched, helplessly as he walked away. Then she swung around to her sisters. "What is wrong with you two?"

"That's funny since I was about to ask you the same thing," Jamie said.

CHAPTER

five

Time was against them. No matter how long Daire worked, he felt as if the hands of time were ticking faster and faster. After two days, he'd managed to trace four of Bran's descendants.

Talin, Neve, and Kyran were checking those offspring who were Fae. Meanwhile, Fintan and Daire had each chosen a mortal family to inspect.

Daire intended to follow another lead. He was veiled when he teleported to Killarney. He remained that way as he walked the streets, getting to know the people and the city.

There were a fair number of tourists, but oddly, few Fae. Why would the Fae steer clear of the area when they didn't do that with any other place in Ireland? It gave him pause, especially since a direct line of Bran's descendants were supposed to live in the area.

He was about to turn away when a flash of color caught his eye. His gaze locked on a woman with a peach plaid flannel shirt and jean-clad legs that went on for days.

She gave a shake of her head, moving the strands of blond hair out of her eyes while she and another woman carried what looked like a part to an engine inside a building.

It wasn't long before she returned, tucking her golden, shoulder-length hair behind her ear and shrugging into a black coat that had seen better days.

She lifted her gaze skyward and looked up at the sun before closing her eyes as if she were soaking in the rays. Before Daire knew it, he was walking toward her. He had no idea what drew him, only that he needed to get a closer look.

Standing five feet from her, he couldn't tear his eyes from the woman. Her heart-shaped face was mesmerizing. With skin almost luminescent, she was a shining light in a sea of dullness. His gaze ran over her incredible cheekbones down to her mouth. Full, tempting lips beckoned him to taste her.

Large eyes so deep a blue they were almost otherworldly lowered and looked around as if searching for something or someone. Without even trying, he'd found a Halfling, and he had a suspicion that she was the descendent he searched for.

Suddenly, her face lit up as a smile pulled at her lips. Daire followed her gaze to find the woman staring at none other than Bran. Daire was so shocked that for a moment he couldn't move. He could only glare in consternation as Bran approached the woman and placed a kiss upon her cheek.

"Hi," she said, smiling up at Bran.

He wrapped an arm around her. "Hi."

Daire was going to be sick. His mind was trying so hard to come to terms with Bran once again beating them to the punch that he didn't listen to the exchange between the Halfling, Bran, and the other woman from earlier who joined them.

It wasn't until the second woman got into a vehicle to drive away that he took in her features. There were similarities enough for him to realize that it was another Halfling and kin to the first.

Daire clenched his fists, the need to lash out at Bran surging through him. He thought of Eoghan, of seeing his friend disappear in the maelstrom of magic. Daire moved closer to Bran and the woman. It was hard to be so near Bran and not attack him, but Daire knew it wouldn't do any good.

He was gaining information for the other Reapers and Erith. And while it killed him not to dole out violence upon Bran, he kept the bigger picture in mind—Bran's death.

Daire kept a healthy distance from Bran's woman in case Bran attempted to see if anyone was veiled around him.

The couple had only gone a few steps before Bran said, "Ettie, it's going to be fine. Jamie just isn't used to you not always being there."

Daire closed his eyes. Damn. Ettie O'Byrne and her sisters, Jamie and Carrie, were exactly who he'd come to find. Without wasting another moment, he returned to Inchmickery and Cael's office.

Cael lowered the map of Ireland he'd been studying and raised a brow. But as soon as he saw Daire's face, concern filled his gaze. "What is it?"

Daire ran a hand down his face. "I found the O'Byrne sisters."

"Then what's the problem?"

He met Cael's gaze. "Bran is already there. He's . . . well, he's inserted himself in the eldest O'Byrne sister's life. I believe he's trying to become her lover."

"You've got to be fekking kidding me." A muscle ticked in Cael's jaw as he hurriedly rolled up the map and tossed it aside before he put his hands on his hips and hung his head.

There were no words to describe how upsetting the situation

was, and Daire didn't even attempt it. Seeing Bran with Ettie was one thing, but actually telling Cael was another kind of abuse he'd rather not go through again.

"You need to get back to Killarney immediately," Cael said.

Daire nodded. "It's my plan."

Cael speared him with his silver eyes. "Find a way into the sister's life. Lie if necessary. We can't let Bran earn her allegiance. Any of the sisters, for that matter."

"I'm not lying to her," Daire announced. "If I do, and I manage to sway her to our side, as soon as she learns the truth—and she will—she'll go to him."

"I don't care how you do it, but stop her from aligning with Bran."

Daire bowed his head and teleported back to Killarney. He was surprised and pleased to discover that the O'Byrne sisters lived in a remote area. It would make things easier if he did run into Bran, which was likely to happen.

Though Daire wanted to know more about Ettie and her relationship with Bran, he remained at the cottage and observed the other two sisters. It allowed his ire time to cool so he could focus on his objective. If he hadn't been so enamored with Ettie, Daire would've known right away that Jamie was a Halfling.

As he watched them, he realized the girls had gotten more than just their beauty from the Fae. Though a few half-Fae had some kind of magic, it was rare.

Daire wouldn't exactly call what the girls had magic, but having Fae blood certainly helped. It allowed Jamie to understand anything mechanical, breaking it down in her mind into the most basic of terms, which then allowed her to fix, build, and rebuild anything.

For Carrie, it was food. She didn't need recipes. She simply saw something in her mind and knew exactly what ingredients were needed, how much of them to use, and how long to cook it.

At the moment, Daire was standing in the kitchen of the homey cottage inhaling the delicious aroma of bread. His mouth watered for a piece, but it wasn't time to show himself to the girls yet.

Instead, he looked around the house. He saw nothing that would give him reason to think the sisters knew they were Halflings. That would make his job more difficult, but he was more than up for the challenge.

He found himself standing in front of a small cabinet. By the look of the wood, it was very old, possibly something passed down through generations. Oddly, it was locked. What could be inside that the O'Byrnes felt the need to hide from others?

Could it be something related to the Fae?

"She's not back," Jamie said angrily as she burst into the house.

Carrie looked over her shoulder as she stirred some ingredients in a bowl. "I don't like him."

"And the more we say that, the more Ettie wants to be around him," Jamie said. She sighed and sank into a chair at the table. "What do we do?"

"Nothing."

Jamie shook her head of long, blond hair. "You're asking the impossible. She's interfered in our lives for as long as I can remember. It's only fair that we do the same with her. Especially because she can't see what we can."

"She won't believe us," Carrie said and set aside the bowl to wipe her hands on her apron as she faced her sister.

Jamie frowned as she cocked her head. "About what? That this Bran guy is a creep? That he makes me want to gag? That there's something really off about him?"

Carrie swallowed hard, her gaze darting to the locked cabinet. Intrigued, Daire moved closer to the girls.

"And why the hell are you looking at the cabinet? You hate that thing," Jamie said.

Carrie took the few steps to the table and put her hands on the back of a chair. "I couldn't sleep last night. The stories Papa told us kept running through my head. So, I snuck into Ettie's room and took the key."

"Well, let me say that I'd be high-fiving you right now for stealing the thing, but I'm more interested in what you did with it."

"I opened the cabinet," Carrie said matter-of-factly. "And I looked through the books."

Jamie shrugged, her face wrinkling in confusion. "What did you hope to find? A picture of Bran labeled Fae?"

Daire's brows shot up. So the girls did know about their ancestry. Good.

"If you're going to act like that, I'm not going to tell you," Carrie announced and turned back to the counter.

Jamie rolled her eyes and blew out a loud sigh. "Fine. I'm sorry, Care. Tell me."

That's all it took for Carrie to whirl back around and yank out a chair across from Jamie to sit. "I was hoping there would be something that told us what a Fae looked like. In all of those books and journals, all it says is that the Fae are so gorgeous they seem not of this world."

"Bran fits that bill," Jamie said, twisting her lips in disgust.

"It's not like we can come out and ask if he's Fae."

Jamie's blue eyes crinkled in the corners as she grinned. "Why not? If he is, he needs to know that we're on to him."

"If only we knew why he was after Ettie."

Daire knew he was taking a chance, but he was gambling on the sisters' love for Ettie and their worry for her when it came to Bran. If he was wrong, everything could be lost.

He moved far back from the girls so they wouldn't feel as threatened and dropped the veil. Almost instantly, their gazes jerked to him as they shot out of their chairs so fast both toppled to the floor.

Daire held his hands up before him, palms out. "Easy. I'm not here to harm you. I'm here to help."

"How?" Jamie demanded.

"I'm a Fae. A Light Fae," he amended.

Carrie quirked a brow and gave him a dark look. "And we're supposed to believe that why?"

"You know you're Halflings, but you know nothing of Fae," he said. "All Fae can use glamour, but without it, the Dark have black and silver hair and red eyes. The more silver, the more evil they've done."

Jamie and Carrie shared a look before Jamie asked, "And the Light?"

"Silver eyes and black hair."

Carrie shook her head. "How do we know you're not using glamour to pretend to be Light?"

"You don't," he said.

Jamie went to the door and opened it. "We don't trust that easily. Get out."

He would have to talk fast in order to gain their trust and assistance. "I ask your forgiveness for eavesdropping, but I came here looking for all of you. I know who Bran is, and he isn't someone any of you should be friends with. I can help get him away."

"Why would you do that?" Jamie demanded.

Daire knew there would be a time to tell them everything because, otherwise, they would never help him. But now wasn't it. "It's a very long story, but suffice it to say that my friends and I have been battling Bran and his army for some time. Your family has been dragged into it because of your connection."

Carrie walked around the table to stand next to Jamie. "Say we believe you. What connection are you talking about?"

"Your family members are direct descendants of Bran's," he told them.

Jamie reached over and took her sister's hand, shock causing her breathing to quicken. "What does that mean?"

"He wants to use you in our war."

Jamie slowly closed the door. "The only reason I'm not forcing you out is because neither Carrie nor I like Bran. We took an instant aversion to him."

"It's because he's Dark," Daire said.

Carrie frowned. "So he's using glamour?"

Daire gave a small shake of his head. "Bran has spent the last several million years in a prison realm called the Netherworld. He was sent there because he turned on the group of men he was with. He divided them, killing some."

"Who sent him to this Netherworld?" Jamie asked.

Daire looked at each of them a long second before he said, "Death."

Jamie's eyes widened. "You're talking about a person."

"I am. Death is the judge and jury of the Fae. My brethren and I are her executioners. Bran was once part of our group, but he broke the rules. Death created the Netherworld and put Bran there for his sins."

"Well," Carrie murmured, her hand at her throat.

Jamie lifted her chin. "All right. How do we get Ettie away from Bran?"

It was just the question Daire hoped they'd ask.

CHAPTER

I t was all a dream. It had to be.

Ettie might like the attention Bran gave her, but it also made her uncomfortable. And she couldn't put her finger on why. Bran was considerate, thoughtful, and more than devoted.

In fact, it was almost too much.

She couldn't believe she was even saying such a thing. Especially after lamenting the fact that no one was interested in her. Now, she didn't like just how much he was? There was something wrong with her. It was the only explanation.

Because anyone else would be over the moon to have a man like Bran courting them. For the last couple of days, he'd taken her to dinner, visited the cottage, they'd gone on walks, and talked.

He asked her dozens of questions about her family and her, but he rarely spoke of himself. Even when she pointedly inquired about something. He always managed to change the subject.

And it didn't help that her sisters were seemingly in an uproar. They made their feelings about her seeing Bran clear. At first, she'd thought they were jealous, but the looks they sent Bran said otherwise.

"Oh, come now," Bran said with a grin as he took her hand while they walked. "Don't let your sisters ruin our day."

Ettie stopped, his words annoying her to the point where she desired to lash out at him. She didn't pull her hand away, though she wanted to. Somehow, she kept her calm. "My sisters are all I have. I need to talk to them and sort this out before it gets worse."

"I've seen the men trailing after them. They're just resentful that I'm not one of them."

She smiled, though it was forced. Ettie didn't know what was wrong with her. Had her sisters' attitudes soured the only romantic interest she'd had in years? She wanted to be furious, but she kept hearing her father's voice in her head, cautioning her while reminding her that family meant everything.

"I know," she replied when Bran looked pointedly at her. "You're right. They're jealous, but I still want to talk to them. We live together, and it's hard on a good day."

Bran took her other hand in his. "Perhaps it's time for them to move out. The land is yours, right?"

"Actually, it's split between all three of us." She wasn't sure why she lied, but the words were past her lips before she could think about why.

A small frown furrowed his brow. "Are you sure?"

"I am. Why would you think otherwise?" If he was interested in her land, she wanted to know the reason.

His fingers tightened on hers slightly. "I just assumed since you were the eldest that it passed to you."

"Let's pick up this conversation later."

"Of course. Let me drive you home. You don't want to have to walk that distance."

In fact, she didn't. "Thank you."

Shortly after, they were in his Range Rover headed toward the O'Byrne cottage. She nodded as Bran talked, but she wasn't listening. She wondered why she was suddenly so wary of him. Had something been said or done to make her so cautious all of a sudden?

All those stories her father told her were turning her against anyone who might give her a bit of happiness. Carrie was right, there was no such thing as a Fae. How could there be when there wasn't a single description of one in all the books and journals her father had?

If her father had met one, he hadn't known it. Otherwise, he'd have made a note of it. And that went for everyone else in the family who had kept the lore alive.

Some families had normal traditions, but not the O'Byrnes. No, they had to believe in the Fae and be ready—though no one said for what.

"You're deep in thought."

She glanced at Bran before looking out over the countryside as they bounced along the dirt road. They crossed the stone bridge that signaled the start of her land.

"Thinking about family," she replied.

He grinned. "Everything's going to be fine. You'll see."

"I hope so."

They didn't speak again until he pulled up at the cottage. Ettie opened the door and was climbing out when he said her name. She looked up into his silver eyes.

"Shall I come in?" he asked hopefully.

She smiled because it was what she was supposed to do. "I don't think it'd be wise for you to be here while I'm talking with my sisters about you."

"True. Shall I ring you later?"

"Of course."

He winked. "Good luck."

Ettie stepped back and shut the door before heading toward the cottage. She paused before the entrance to the house and took a deep breath as the engine of the vehicle roared before Bran drove away. Then she walked inside.

As usual, Carrie was in the kitchen, cooking. Her youngest sister looked Ettie's way and flashed her a quick smile. "Hi."

"Hey." Ettie closed the door behind her. "Where's Jamie?"

Carrie motioned behind her with her hand. "Out in the garage, I'm sure."

It wasn't that Ettie wanted to have a confrontation with her sisters, but to get worked up for exactly that and then come home to . . . nothing . . . was, well, disconcerting.

She left the house and went to the shed Jamie used as her garage. Ettie found her sister on her back beneath a car so that only her bent legs were visible.

"I want to talk to you about Bran," Ettie said.

Jamie set aside a wrench and grabbed another tool from the ground beside her. "Then talk."

"I'd rather do it when I can see your face."

"I'm busy," Jamie replied. "If you have something to say, then say it."

Ettie looked back at the cottage and the window into the kitchen where she saw Carrie moving about.

"You usually wait to do this at dinner, but I'm guessing you don't want Carrie and me ganging up on you," Jamie said.

Ettie briefly closed her eyes, irritation causing her hackles to rise. "Why do you have to make everything so difficult?"

"I'm not. It was an observation. A correct one, at that. Just admit it."

Ettie hated that she couldn't see Jamie's face. Her voice was calm, belying the anger she was certain Jamie couldn't keep from her expression. But Ettie couldn't be sure.

"Fine. I don't want you two to side against me. Is that what you want to hear?" she asked.

Jamie scooted from beneath the car to look at her. "Yes."

Ettie opened her mouth to speak when Jamie moved back underneath the car. It was useless to ask her to remain. Jamie would do whatever Jamie wanted to do. It had been that way since she was old enough to crawl.

"I need to know something," Ettie said. "The truth."

There was a snort from beneath the car. "I always give you the truth."

"I want to know if you dislike Bran, or if you don't like the idea of me with someone."

Jamie was out from beneath the car so quickly that Ettie had to jump back to avoid her sister slamming into her shins. She gaped at Jamie, but it was the fury she saw in her sister's soft blue eyes that made her hold her tongue.

"How dare you," Jamie said as she sat up. "Do you honestly think I'm so shallow that I'd begrudge you having a man? Of all the things you could've said!"

Ettie held up her hands. "To be fair, that's exactly how it seemed at first. Carrie wouldn't acknowledge me at the pub until Bran sat down with me. Then she was suddenly there. Same with you when we walked out of the bar that night. You always ignore me on your dates, but suddenly I have a man with me, and you can't stay away."

For long minutes, Jamie merely stared at her. Then her sister got to her feet and threw down the wrench she'd been holding before storming out.

Ettie glanced at the tool. Jamie never flung her tools. Every one was carefully wiped clean each day and put away. For her to toss it aside like that meant she was furious.

But so was Ettie.

Whether Jamie wanted to admit it or not, both she and Carrie had been all smiles with Bran for . . . Ettie's thoughts ground to a halt as she realized somewhere over the last few days her sisters had stopped grinning at Bran and began scowling.

Jamie and Carrie were a lot of things, but the one thing none of them had ever done was fight over a man. Ettie felt like a fool for believing her sisters wanted Bran. Of course, the thought had been put there by Bran himself.

Ettie walked from the garage back into the house and straight to her room where she changed into a tracksuit and running shoes. A long jog and fresh air would help to clear her head—hopefully.

"I'll be back later," Ettie said to Carrie as she left the house.

Without looking around, she headed toward the stream and the trail that followed it all the way to the mountain. It was her favorite place to run. At first, the exercise had been an excuse to leave the cottage and get some alone time. It wasn't long after that it became a much-loved habit.

Ettie pushed herself hard, running full-out all the way to the mountain, and she didn't pause to rest before starting the climb up the winding, twisting trail up to the top.

When she reached the summit, she stopped and bent over, her hands on her knees as she gulped in air while the frigid wind cooled her heated flesh. But there was a smile on her face. Her body always felt great after exertion. Jamie joked that it was a substitute for sex—and it was.

Her training had also been done because Ettie wanted to be ready for whatever her father believed would come for either them or their children. Ettie straightened and put her hands on her hips as she looked around.

For so long, she'd believed every word her father told her. It was only now that she began to doubt him. How she hated that he wasn't around for her to question and debate things with. His conviction in the Fae had been so strong that it lasted five years after his death.

Five years that she had been taking care of her sisters and the land. Five years where she dedicated everything to training for a supposed event that may or may not occur.

How many of her ancestors had done the same thing? How many others watched the years pass them by as they held to their beliefs with such certainty that they died for it?

More importantly, did she want to be a casualty to this . . . whatever it was?

"What do I do?" she asked the air. She threw out her arms and lifted her face to the sky. "What do I do?!"

Her arms fell to her sides as she lowered her head. How could she have been so certain of things for so long, and now doubt everything?

"What do you do about what?"

The sound of the male voice startled her, causing her to jerk around. She found him with one leg braced on the summit as he paused on the trail, a black brow quirked.

Ettie opened her mouth, but there were no words as she took in the sight of him. He was . . . beautiful in a rugged, untamed way that made her heart race and her stomach quiver.

It became impossible to breathe as she drank in the cut of his jaw and square chin. She tried not to stare at his mouth and thick bottom lip, but all she could think about was what it would be like to kiss him. Then she looked into his eyes.

They were molten silver, dark and enigmatic like mercury. And those gorgeous eyes framed with long, black lashes watched her with the concentration of a hawk.

Layers of thick ebony hair fell nearly to his shoulders with the top half of it pulled away from his face. He wore only a denim shirt with a cream tee beneath it and faded jeans and black boots. She didn't know how he was up there without a coat.

His lips slowly pulled into a smile, and she realized she'd been ogling him. Ettie glanced away, but her gaze returned immediately. She laughed nervously, still unable to find words.

"I didn't mean to interrupt," he said as he took the last step to the top. "I assumed since you shouted your question, you might want an answer."

His Irish brogue was deep, throaty, and absolutely sexy. It was slightly different than anything she'd heard before, and she wanted more.

"Do you have an answer to my question?" she asked.

He looked around and shrugged. "Well, that depends on exactly what you're talking about."

"Are you sure you want to know?"

"I believe I do."

She smiled, wondering if he was her father's answer to her question. Either way, she was about to find out.

CHAPTER

seven

Never had so much depended on his next words. Daire hadn't known when the right time to approach Ettie would be, and he hadn't intended to do it when he followed her on her run. But then she'd shouted her question—and it seemed the right thing to do.

Her sisters were so willing to get Ettie far from Bran that they trusted Daire. He wasn't going to let them down, nor would he allow Ettie to fall into whatever trap Bran had waiting for her.

"You're on my land," she said, with the edges of her mouth still curved into a grin.

Daire wrinkled his nose. "My apologies."

"There are some hikers who come this way, but since you don't have a backpack, I'm guessing you're not one of them."

He gave a shake of his head. "I saw you running up the mountain. It's an impressive feat to do with such speed. I wanted to meet you. I'm Daire."

"Ettie," she replied. She shivered and wrapped her arms around her. "You're not cold?"

"No. Shall we go down?"

She stared at him a long minute before she said, "I like the privacy up here. Besides, I'm curious about you."

"And here I thought you only wanted me to stay to answer your question."

"Right," she said with a laugh.

The sound hit him right in the chest, taking his breath for a moment. He wanted to tuck her blond hair behind her ear, but he remained where he was.

She tilted her head, her deep blue eyes pinning him. "This isn't like me at all."

"Sometimes, it's good to break out of our molds and do something different."

"Yeah." Her head turned to the side as she looked out over the land. "I've lived in this one place my entire life. I used to play up here. I'd pretend I was a queen, and all of this before me was my kingdom."

He eyed the landscape. "It's certainly picture-perfect for just such an imagination."

She swallowed and wrapped her arms around herself. "If you're going to give me an answer to my question, you need details."

"That would be helpful."

Throwing him a quick grin, she said, "My father had special interests that were passed down through the family. He, in turn, gave them to my sisters and me. He spent his entire life chasing after answers, never to find any."

"Is that what you're doing? Chasing answers?"

"Actually, no." She looked at him. "I accepted everything my father told me as gospel. I did what he wanted, even after his untimely death. But now . . . now, I've begun questioning whether he was off his rocker and if any of it is real."

Daire knew this was about the Fae. He could tell her all of it right then, but he wasn't so sure that would be the wise choice. If Ettie doubted things, then she needed to come back to it slowly, or he might lose her altogether.

"Something made you begin questioning what your father told you," he said.

She twisted her lips ruefully. "It's something my sister said. I don't even remember what it was, but it struck a chord and caused me to reevaluate everything."

"Sometimes, doing that can allow you to see things more clearly."

After a loud snort, she said, "I've been in training since I was four years old."

"Training?"

"To fight. I can use just about any weapon you put in front of me, but my specialty is hand-to-hand combat."

He shifted his stance, more intrigued by the minute. "What were you training for?"

"That's just it. I don't know. My father just kept telling me I needed to be ready."

"And he never told you why?"

She shook her head as the breeze briefly lifted the strands of her hair. "Never. I don't think he knew. He'd been told that same narrative, and I believe it's been passed down through generations."

"Which is why your question came to be."

She blew out a breath. "Exactly."

"What do you want to do?"

Her deep blue eyes swung to him. "I thought you were going to give me an answer?"

"Maybe the answer comes with the question." His heart skipped a beat when she smiled, the corners of her eyes crinkling. By the stars, she was beautiful. "What do you want to do?"

"I want to be normal."

Daire didn't have the heart to tell her that as a Halfling, her life would be anything but.

"I want . . ." she paused, a frown forming on her brow. "I don't know what I want." She laughed and shook her head as she lowered herself onto a boulder. "My father set a course before me, and I've always been on it."

He straddled a rock and lowered himself down to sit. "I gather your sisters don't have these questions?"

"Oh, no. Both want to leave as soon as they can."

"So, you feel as if your father's legacy rests solely on you."

Fathomless blue eyes stared at him. "Yes. Who are you?"

"You wouldn't believe me if I told you."

"Try me," she demanded.

Daire looked down at his hands. He was gambling once again. He'd always been a bit of a rogue, his rebellious streak creating all sorts of havoc. Once he became a Reaper, he'd learned to control it for the most part.

He'd dipped his toe into things again with the O'Byrne sisters, but being so near Ettie, he was fast losing the will to govern that particular trait.

"Daire," she urged.

The sound of his name on her lips did strange things to his body. Desire grew as need roared within him—loudly and fiercely. He fisted his hands so he wouldn't reach over and haul her atop his lap so he could ravage her lips.

He finally met her gaze. A dozen words came to mind, but only two passed his lips. "I'm Fae."

She didn't laugh or gasp in outrage. She simply stared at him for a long, silent minute. Then she rose, and without a word, started down the mountain path.

Daire slowly stood, his gaze never leaving her. Perhaps this was the time to be the more cautious Reaper he'd become over the centuries instead of his old self, the one who left everything to chance. He didn't know what had come over him, and he wasn't sure how to fix it.

He walked to the edge and looked down the slope to continue watching Ettie make her way down the path. Suddenly, she stopped and whirled around. Then she marched back up the mountain until she was a few feet from him.

Her deep blue eyes blazed with fury. "Is this some joke? Something Carrie put you up to?"

"No."

"Sure," she said with a huff and spun back around.

Before she got two steps from him, Daire teleported in front of her, causing her to stumble backward at their near collision so that she fell back, catching herself on one hand before her butt could land on the ground.

The anger evaporated, as her eyes grew large with amazement —and, sadly, a bit of fear.

"I won't hurt you," he told her and took a couple of steps away to give her space. "But I am Fae."

She pushed herself into a standing position and dusted her hand off on her leg. "What do you want?"

"I want to keep you safe."

"No." She held his gaze, her chin rising. "You waited until now to show yourself, and that's because you want something."

"Do you have any idea how many Halflings there are? We can't keep up with all of them."

She raised a brow. "But you knew about my sisters and me."

"Only because we searched for you."

"Because you want something," she stated flatly.

Daire took a deep breath and released it, reluctance causing him to hesitate. He saw her shiver as she stood her ground. "Let's get you inside."

"I'm fine."

"Don't be stubborn. I see you trembling. The temperatures would have to be much worse before I'm affected, but you'll only hurt yourself by remaining out here."

She blew out a harsh breath and walked around him as she mumbled, "You're insufferable."

At least she was talking to him.

Daire followed her down into the valley. By the time they reached the cottage, Jamie was outside with a steaming mug in her hand. She handed it to Ettie as she walked into the house.

"Well?" Jamie whispered to him.

He shrugged. "It didn't go as I'd hoped."

She rolled her eyes. "Nothing ever does with my sister. Come in."

Following Jamie inside the cottage, he found a plate shoved at him from Carrie. The sweet smell was too delicious to even ask what it was. He took a bite and savored the way the morsel melted in his mouth, exploding with flavors of vanilla, cinnamon, and nutmeg.

"This is amazing," he said after swallowing.

Carrie beamed. "Are you hungry? I could make you whatever you want."

"He won't be staying that long," Ettie replied when she walked out of her room. "Obviously, you two have already met Daire. I also gather that you know what he is."

Daire's gaze swung to her. Ettie had changed into dark jeans and a pastel blue sweater that made him take notice of her eyes even more. She ran her hands through her short locks.

"Yes," her sisters answered in unison.

There would be no pleasantries with Ettie. It was probably for the best. The sooner the O'Byrne sisters knew about the entire threat, the sooner they could make up their minds. Though he wasn't entirely sure they would side with the Reapers. Yet, what other choice did he have?

He couldn't continue to allow Bran to get closer to Ettie. The Halfling needed to know just who was wooing her. And why.

Daire set down the plate and licked his lips. "You were partly right up on the mountain. I did seek your family out, but not to bring harm. I'm trying to steer you from it."

"Bran," Jamie said.

He gave a nod to the middle O'Bryne sister. "Bran isn't who he claims to be."

"He's not claimed to be anything," Ettie replied acerbically.

Carrie made a sound at the back of her throat. "That's a lie. He claims to be human."

"Well, he didn't actually say that," Ettie said. She sat in one of the two chairs and motioned Daire to the sofa.

He walked into the living area and took the far corner of the couch while Jamie sank into the other chair and Carrie curled up in the other corner of the sofa.

"By not telling you he was Fae, Bran lied," Daire pointed out.

Ettie crossed one long leg over the other. "I'll give you that. Perhaps you should start at the beginning."

"The beginning." Daire leaned forward so that his forearms

rested on his knees. He clasped his hands together and lowered his gaze to the ground. "You three have lived life knowing you had Fae blood in your veins. There are thousands more who don't know their heritage. I'm not sure if it's better to know or not."

Jamie crossed her arms over her middle. "Things would've been much simpler for me had I not known."

"Ditto," Carrie said.

Daire slid his gaze to Ettie, who didn't reply. She sat silently, waiting for him to continue. He briefly pressed his lips together. "What I'm about to tell you isn't to be taken lightly. In fact, if a Fae heard this, they would have to be killed immediately."

"We'll be spared? Why? Because we're part human?" Carrie asked.

He glanced at her and lifted one shoulder in a shrug. "Something like that. The fact is, you weren't raised with the Fae, but the real reason is that unless you know what's going on, you can't make an informed decision. I believe that's why Death has given us leave to impart this information to Halflings."

"Death?" Ettie asked in a soft voice.

Jamie quickly said, "Yes. A person. Go on," she urged Daire.

He looked at each of them, meeting Ettie's gaze last. "I work for Death. I told your sisters that Death is judge and jury. My brethren and I are the executioners. Death keeps the balance within the Fae. We don't meddle in mortal affairs."

"What about Halflings, as you call us?" Carrie asked.

Daire shook his head. "You live in the mortal world."

"Until a Fae comes to meddle," Ettie stated. "Right?"

He slowly straightened and sat back. "Yes."

CHAPTER
eight

One word turned her ire to trepidation. One simple utterance that spoke volumes.

Ettie didn't want to hear whatever it was Daire had to say because she knew her world was about to be turned on its ear. And she wasn't ready.

Then again, was anyone ever?

She took slow breaths to calm her racing heart. Mercurial eyes fastened on her. No matter how she tried, she couldn't look away from Daire. She wanted to hate him for showing up now, for being nice, and because she was wildly attracted to him. A kind of allure she had never experienced before.

Yet she couldn't bring herself to feel such animosity.

Her father had looked for Fae his entire life. If only he had lived, he could've met two.

"I'm a Reaper," Daire announced. "Each of us is chosen by Death. And at one time, Bran was one of us, as well. That ended when he broke the rules."

Carrie released her hair from its ponytail and rubbed her scalp. "What kind of rules?"

"The biggest I already told you. No Fae can know of us. If they learn who the Reapers are, they have to be killed," he said.

Jamie asked, "Why? What does it matter?"

Each time her sisters posed a question, Daire looked at them, but his gaze always returned to Ettie. It was almost as if his story was just for her.

"It matters," Daire said. "The Fae grow up with tales of Reapers. The Light use the stories as a way to prevent their children from turning Dark. The Dark tell them to scare their kids into acting how they want."

When he paused, Ettie folded her hands in her lap. "And?"

"None of the Fae know the Reapers are real. We're a myth to them, legends," he explained. "Each of us died. That's how Death found us, chose us. So to keep our identities a secret—as well as what we do—we leave everything and everyone we knew and loved behind."

"Damn," Jamie murmured.

Daire shrugged. "For some of us, it isn't a problem. We only have each other. There are no relationships for any of us. But there are times, like now, where we're sent to either investigate or find someone. We have to blend in, but we always keep our true identities a secret from the Fae. Bran didn't do that. He fell in love with a Light Fae and told her who and what he was."

"It resulted in her death," Ettie surmised.

Daire bowed his head in acknowledgement. "Bran went crazy afterward. He divided the Reapers and attacked, killing the leader. By the time the fighting ended, there were only three left of the seven. Bran, Cael, and Eoghan."

"Why didn't Death step in?" Carrie inquired.

"Death did. Cael and Eoghan wanted Bran dead, but Death created a prison realm called the Netherworld and threw Bran there. And that's where he remained for eons until he managed to escape."

It didn't take a lot for Ettie to realize what Bran wanted. "He's motivated by revenge."

Daire glanced out the window. "He began his plan by slaughtering thousands of Halflings all over the world. Then he attacked any of them that we managed to save."

"What for?" Ettie asked. "If most Halflings don't know what they are, how can they pose a threat to him?"

Daire leaned back on the sofa, his lips flattening briefly. "We're still working that out. But we have learned that, somehow, Bran is stealing Death's magic."

"What a slime," Jamie muttered in disgust.

Daire gave her a half-smile. "He's linked to Death because of it, which prevents him from finding Death, and Death from locating him. It's also why none of the Reapers can kill anyone in his army."

"He has an army?" Ettie asked, a sinking feeling pressing against her chest.

"He's recruiting from within the Dark Fae."

Ettie nodded in shock. "Oh."

What else did one say to such a statement?

"We found there's a loophole, however," Daire said.

Carrie eagerly sat forward. "What? What did you discover?"

"There is a family in Galway who have had not one, but three different Fae impregnate women over the generations. They are the most powerful Halflings in the realm. Bran tried to recruit one of the last remaining members of the family—Catriona. But Cat fought him. You see, her powers give her the ability to call anyone or anything to her. Bran wanted her to bring him Death. Then, he wanted Cat to kill Death."

Jamie propped her elbow on the chair before dropping her head into her hand. "How did Cat stop him?"

"Because the Reapers were part of Death's army, we couldn't harm him. But that didn't apply to Cat. She wounded him but, unfortunately, Bran got away before Cat could end this chaos he began."

Ettie uncrossed her legs and fought the need to pace. After all the years of not seeing a Fae, she was getting information overload, and it was freaking her out. "That brought you to us."

Daire ran a hand down his face. "That it did. But I need to backtrack some. When the Halflings were attacked, and we stepped in, Baylon, one of my fellow Reapers, fell in love with Jordyn, one of those we were sent to protect. Death could see that history was repeating itself, so adjustments were made to the rules. No Fae can know about us, that didn't change, but Jordyn risked her very life to save Death. That allowed Jordyn and Baylon to be together."

"Please tell me there's more," Jamie said with a grin.

He chuckled and nodded his head of dark hair. "There's River, another Halfling. She has the power to read and understand all Fae dialects. Most importantly, ones that have been dead for eons. She was collecting a set of texts that were of Fae origin, and she kept them locked away in the Edinburgh library where she worked. We managed to convince her to help us right before Bran tried to steal the books from her. In the process, she and Kyran fell in love. She's now expecting his child."

"Death allowed her to live because of the child?" Ettie asked.

"Actually, Death allowed River to live because she translates the texts we need," Daire explained.

Carrie shot her a dark look before grinning at Daire. "Any more?"

Ettie sighed loudly. Both of her sisters were hopeless romantics who let the world know it. She was one, as well, but she kept it to herself. No need to make herself worse off than she already was.

"There are Talin and Neve," Daire said. "Talin was sent to spy on the Light Court, but he fell for Neve. Neve is full Fae. Bran knew of Talin and Neve's connection and killed Neve's parents, then turned her brother Dark."

Ettie's stomach plummeted to her feet. She looked at her sisters, her mind rioting at the thought of losing them in such a way.

"Neve's life was ended by her brother," Daire continued.

Ettie wasn't sure how much more she could take. She tore her gaze away from Daire, wishing she could stop his words, as well. Yet, she wouldn't. As hard as they were to hear, she wanted to know them.

The silence that stretched pulled her eyes back to Daire. Only when their gazes met did he continue.

"I told you each Reaper died, but I didn't say that we were all betrayed in some way. When Neve's brother deceived and killed her, Death gave Neve a choice. Neve became a Reaper that day. But we lost Eoghan, another of us. In the battle with Bran, a Light Fae named Rhi stepped in to help us. The mix of magic created a storm that Bran directed at Cael."

Jamie lifted her head, a frown furrowing her brow. "Cael? Why him?"

"He's our leader. He and Eoghan were the two left from the original Reapers, and Bran wants nothing more than to kill them. He tried to take out Cael, but Eoghan pushed him out of the way and was swallowed by the magic instead."

Ettie curled her fingers into a fist at the strong urge to reach out to Daire and comfort him. "I'm sorry."

"Eoghan isn't dead," Daire stated. "We just have to find him. He could be on any of the numerous realms."

Carrie whistled, her eyebrows raised. "You're looking for Eoghan and fighting Bran."

"That's quite a load," Jamie said.

Daire ran a hand along his jaw. "Cat is with the Reapers now because she stood with us and Death, which is good because she and Fintan are together. Needless to say, when Bran learned that some of the Reapers had lovers, his anger ballooned."

"You still haven't said how we fit in," Jamie stated.

"I was getting to that."

Once more, his silver eyes returned to Ettie. It made her feel as if it were just the two of them in the room. She didn't know how long they stared at each other. Time ceased to exist. It was just her and the enigmatic Fae with the mouth-watering face and eyes that could make her melt.

Daire scooted to the edge of the cushion and leaned forward, bracing his arms on his legs. "It was by happenstance that River found something in one of the ancient Fae texts. It was a mention of a family, Ó Broin, which means descendants of Bran."

"So?" Carrie asked.

But Ettie understood. Only because she'd done research on her family for a project in school. "O'Byrne is the Anglicized spelling of Ó Broin," she told her sisters. To Daire, she asked, "You're telling us we're descended from him?"

Daire's head moved up and down in affirmation.

Ettie jumped to her feet, no longer able to control her need to move. She paced the area, inwardly screaming. She didn't know what it meant, but it couldn't be good.

She turned, and Daire was before her. He put his hands on her arms to keep her still. When he did, something warm and thrilling charged through her.

"Bran had three children with his Fae wife before he became a Reaper," Daire said after a moment. Then he reluctantly released her. "He also had two offspring with mortals. I traced one of those lines to you."

Jamie got to her feet and came to stand with them. "We can't be his only descendants who are alive."

"You aren't," Daire said, glancing at her. "My brethren are checking the others."

Carrie pulled her knees up to her chest while still on the sofa. "But Bran is here."

"Which means, he wants us," Ettie said and looked at Daire.

His arm reached out for her, but before he made contact, Daire let it drop to his side. "I think so, but I don't know why. It can't be good, whatever the reason."

"He asked if I owned the land today," she said. Ettie ignored her sisters' chagrined looks and focused instead on Daire. "I lied and told him it was split between all three of us. He then asked me if I was sure."

"Then it must have something to do with this cottage or the land," Carrie said.

Daire asked, "Why did you lie to him?"

Ettie shrugged helplessly. "I don't know. It was just a feeling I got."

"I'm glad you listened to your instincts."

So was she. Ettie grew uncomfortable and looked away, only to find her gaze clashing with Jamie, who was grinning at her.

"I know what I want to cook tonight," Carrie said as she jumped up. "I'm going to head into town to get supplies."

Ettie immediately said, "Not on your own, you're not."

"I got this," Jamie said, still grinning.

It wasn't until the two exchanged a conspiratorial look and walked from the house that Ettie realized she was now alone with Daire. Her eyes swiveled to his to find him staring at her.

No words were spoken as the engine roared to life and Jamie and Carrie drove away. Ettie knew the best thing to do would be to put some distance between her and Daire. Being so close to him was making her feel . . . all sorts of wanton, lustful things.

But her feet wouldn't move.

"Bran will be back for you," he said.

She nodded slowly. "I'll send him away."

"It's going to take a lot more than that. You're going to need me."

Why did those words cause an image of her bed to flash in her head? Tangled limbs, heavy breathing, sweat-slicked skin.

"That is, if you want my help," Daire added, jerking her out of her thoughts.

"I'd be a fool to turn you away."

His smile was slow, and entirely too sexy. "And you certainly aren't a fool."

That was debatable. She had fallen for Bran's charm at first, after all. Thankfully, it hadn't lasted.

She knew that there were no guarantees in life, and with Bran's attention on them, anything could happen. All the years of filling the role of mother as well as sister had her thoughts turning to her siblings.

"I want a promise from you," she told Daire.

The smile was gone, his expression intense. "What would that be?"

"Eventually, Bran will realize I lied about the land being mine. I'll fight him—"

"And I'll be beside you," Daire interrupted.

She shook her head and moved closer to him. He had to understand how important this was to her. "I want you to take Jamie and Carrie. Take them somewhere far away, where Bran can never find them. Promise me," she insisted.

He searched her gaze before he tucked her hair behind her ear and whispered, "I promise, Ettie."

CHAPTER
nine

The vow was sealed with his words. Daire couldn't go back on it, and he knew that would come back to haunt him. He remained still when Ettie walked around him.

His head followed her progress, his senses drinking in the smell of clover and wind that was her scent. Though he saw the trepidation in her eyes, she hid it from her sisters well.

It was easy to see that as the eldest, she carried the burden of most everything. Jamie and Carrie had become so accustomed to it that they didn't realize they put added stress on Ettie by not picking up the slack.

"I wonder if this is what my father wanted me to be ready for," Ettie said as she opened the fridge. After glancing inside, she shut it and looked around as if trying to find something to do.

Daire turned her way and leaned a shoulder against the wall. "You say you know how to fight."

"It's the one thing I'm good at."

He could argue the point that she was good at other things like managing her sisters and the estate, but he didn't. "Care to show me?"

"You just want to take my mind off things."

"Maybe. Or maybe I want to see what you can do."

Deep blue eyes narrowed on him. Without another word, she walked to him and threw a punch.

Daire leaned to the side and raised his arms to block her. He then grabbed her wrist, turning so that he had her back against him. She elbowed him and twisted, sliding out of his hold.

She was quick, agile, and slippery as an eel. What began as an exercise, soon turned into a battle of wills as they moved from room to room.

He didn't use his full strength—yet. They would build up to that, but he was impressed with her skills, just the same. If she had a Fae weapon, she could inflict untold damage on Bran—or any Fae for that matter.

They were both breathing hard, a sheen of sweat glistening on Ettie's face when Daire spun her and pinned her between a wall and his body.

Their eyes clashed.

And desire swelled.

Just as he was about to release her, Ettie briefly looked at his mouth. That's all it took for his control to snap.

He gazed at her. The need he saw in her expression made blood rush to his cock. He flattened his hand on the wall near her face and leaned closer.

She released his shirt and put her palms on his chest. Her breathing grew ragged for an entirely different reason.

With her lips parted, she lifted her face to his. It was wrong to mix pleasure with business, but Daire didn't care. He wanted Ettie.

Craved her, actually. It wasn't one-sided either. And that's what ultimately made his decision.

He lowered his head, their lips briefly meeting. Heat sizzled between them. He dropped an arm to her hips and gripped her as he pressed his body close.

Her quick intake of breath told him she felt his arousal. Then she sighed and planted her hands on either side of his head as if to make sure he didn't stop kissing her. He began to deepen the kiss when he heard a car door.

Ettie's head jerked to the side as she peered out the window. Daire saw that it was Bran the same time she did.

"What the hell?" she murmured.

He grabbed her shoulders and made her look at him. "Don't tell him I'm here, and don't let on that you know who he is."

"Why?" she whispered.

Daire gave her a quick kiss. "Later. I'll be here the entire time." Then he stepped back and veiled himself.

"Daire?" she called.

He touched her arm. "I'm here. Just veiled."

She relaxed before straightening her clothes and smoothing back her hair. A moment later, Bran knocked on the door. After counting to ten, she walked to the entrance and opened it.

"Hi," Bran said with a bright smile.

She returned it. "Hi."

"I wanted to see how things went with your sisters."

"We've only begun our discussion. Nothing has been determined yet," Ettie told him.

Daire saw how Bran looked around. No doubt the bastard was trying to determine if any Reapers were there. Daire wouldn't leave her, but by remaining, he was taking a chance that Bran would find him.

Lowering himself to the ground might work, but it might not. He could go to the roof, but there was a chance that would fail, as well. The only place he knew would work was right next to Ettie.

He teleported right behind her, wrapping his arms around her waist as he leaned his mouth close to her ear and whispered, "Act natural."

Bran motioned inside with his hand. "May I come in?"

"It really isn't a good time," she said.

"The car is gone. I gather your sisters are, as well."

Ettie stared at him for a long moment. "They went to pick up some things for dinner so we could finish our talk."

"Then we have a few minutes. I won't stay long."

She moved so he could enter.

It rankled Daire that Bran was inside the cottage, but Daire asked her not to let Bran know anything. Ettie had no choice but to allow him entrance.

Bran bent at the kitchen table and smelled some of the treats Carrie had left out. Then he looked at Ettie. "Are you all right?"

"I'm not, actually."

"So things aren't going well with your sisters?"

She leaned back against Daire. He held her tightly, felt her pulse racing.

Ettie shrugged one shoulder. "It's not something that will be sorted out quickly. This could take days."

"I'm sorry to hear that," Bran said as he clasped his hands behind his back. "I don't understand why they can't allow you to have some happiness."

She held his gaze. "I don't know."

"You said they're almost ready to leave. Perhaps it's time they did."

Ettie gaped at him. "You can't be serious? They're my sisters, my family."

"Who are holding you back," Bran argued. "Do they help you around the house? You do everything for them. You've given up so much to raise them and be a surrogate mother when you were just a child yourself."

Daire bit back a growl. Bran was right on all accounts, but it galled him that Bran said it. It was obvious that Bran wanted something at the cottage, but Daire had yet to figure out what it was. Ettie, however, was merely a means to an end for Bran.

That, in turn, pleased Daire and infuriated him. Because that meant that as soon as Ettie became irrelevant, Bran would likely kill her.

Daire wasn't surprised when Bran lifted his hand and swung it away around him, magic filling the air as he searched for Reapers.

"A man begins to court you, and where are your sisters when you try to talk? Gone. I knew I should've stayed," Bran said.

"This is our business. Not yours," Ettie replied tightly.

Bran's face crumpled in fake hurt. "You wound me. I thought we had something special."

"I'm not saying we don't," she argued. "What I'm saying is that even if you were my husband, this is something between my sisters and me and no one else."

He bowed his head and gave her a small smile. "I just don't want them taking advantage of you. They've done enough."

"I don't mind."

"You do," he pressed. "I saw you sitting alone in the pub while Carrie was surrounded by men and Jamie was out on a date. I saw how, as soon as Carrie spotted me with you, she was at the table, flirting."

Daire hadn't known any of that. He hated that Bran had been

there and used what was obviously a low moment with Ettie to get close. Daire tightened his arms around her, offering what small comfort he could.

"So you pitied me," Ettie fired back.

Bran's brows snapped together. "I never said that."

"You implied it. Did you think I was so lonely that I'd jump at any man who flashed me a smile?"

"No."

"You're damn right I wouldn't."

Daire felt her tremble again, but this time, it was with rage. Her breathing came in huffs as she glared at Bran.

Instead of being put off, Bran smiled. "Ah, the fire within you is a glorious thing. It's your spirit that drew me to you."

Daire had to bite back a retort that nearly passed his lips. He'd cautioned Ettie, perhaps he should've given himself that same talk.

She blew out a breath and covered her face with her hands before slowly running them downward. "I don't know what to say to that."

"There's no need to reply," Bran said. "You look as if you could use a nice dinner. Let me take you out. I'll make you forget all about this thing with your sisters."

"Why?"

Both Daire and Bran frowned at her. Daire had no idea what she was getting at, and he grew nervous as silence followed her question.

Finally, Bran asked, "Why, what?"

"Why do you want me?"

Bran chuckled and moved closer. "I believe I've told you multiple times. Why is it so hard for you to understand how desirable you are?"

"I just want to make sure it's me you want and not something else."

"What else is there but you?" Bran asked.

Daire had to admit that Bran said all the right things. No wonder Ettie had melted under that charm. Bran was as smooth as silk.

She smiled up at Bran and even rested her hand on his chest. "The offer of dinner sounds lovely, but I don't think I'd be very good company tonight. How about tomorrow?"

"I'll take you out anytime you want, but I wish you'd change your mind about tonight."

Ettie shook her head. "It wouldn't be fair to you. I've already let my temper get the best of me and directed it towards you when you were just showing me compassion."

"If I can't change your mind, then perhaps I should stay," he offered.

Daire wanted to throw him out of the house himself. Couldn't Bran take a hint?

"Not until I get this thing settled with my sisters," Ettie said. "And I will. Soon."

"I'll hold you to that," Bran said.

Ettie moved to the door and opened it. "I'll have everything in order in a few days. I promise."

"A man can't ask for more than that." Bran then walked to her. He paused and gazed down. "Is it just your sisters bothering you?"

"It's only been the three of us for a while now. And I hate having dissention. When something isn't resolved, it tears me up inside. It doesn't help that they hate confrontation, so I have to work extra hard."

"Do you want to?"

Ettie cocked her head to the side. "Do I want to talk to my sisters? Yes."

"Work for this? For us," he clarified.

She gave him a hurt look. "If I didn't, would I continue seeing you?"

"Very true," he said after a long hesitation.

"You don't believe me."

Bran flashed her a tight smile. "I usually get what I want, and right now, my sights are set on you. I don't like that your sisters are coming between us."

"They aren't coming between us. I won't allow that," Ettie quickly said.

Even Daire got the distinct impression that Bran had given a veiled threat. Perhaps it was time to bring in more Reapers to watch over Carrie and Jamie.

Bran's smile widened as he gave her a wink. "Until tomorrow."

"Until tomorrow," she replied.

Bran gave her a kiss on the cheek before leaving.

CHAPTER

ten

Something was amiss. Bran knew it, but he couldn't lay his finger on what it might be. He'd sent out a blast of magic to see if any Reapers were near and veiled, but there had been nothing. Yet, there was no doubt Ettie was acting differently.

Bran pulled up at the manor he had chosen for himself and got out of the Range Rover. He walked to Searlas, who stood, waiting outside.

"I know that look," his second in command said.

Bran stopped before him and rubbed his jaw. "I thought the Reapers might've discovered what we were about."

"They're not that smart."

He exchanged a grin with Searlas. "Don't underestimate Death or Cael. However, I'm happy to report that we can proceed with our plans. I believe Ettie might need some coaxing, though. She's developed a case of cold feet where I'm concerned."

"But you've been in the cottage."

"That means nothing. I need her not only on my side, but I

require her consent, as well. Otherwise, all of this has been for naught."

"Then we get her on our side before the Reapers show up," Searlas said.

Bran knew it wouldn't be easy to turn Ettie, but he hadn't imagined her sisters getting in the way. Ettie was the secret to everything. Once he had her, he had the sisters, the land, and more importantly, the key to the cabinet.

"What's next?" Searlas asked.

"I allow Ettie a little more time with Jamie and Carrie. If the two siblings don't come around, then I'll send you and another in to . . . persuade the girls."

Searlas grinned, his red eyes alight with anticipation. "Why wait? I'd like a taste of the youngest."

"One more day, and then she's all yours."

Searlas rubbed his hands together.

Bran walked past his lieutenant and entered the house. The estate had been remolded and boasted the clean lines of a minimalist design, while the furniture and rugs had been recovered from bygone years.

The manor wasn't exactly his tastes, but his sights were set on something larger—the entire universe. Once Death was gone, Bran could live wherever he wanted. Perhaps he'd even take the Light Castle.

Or build himself another.

Unlike Erith, he wouldn't hide on another realm. He would live in the middle of the realm the Fae had chosen, to remind all beings of his power. And reach.

They would fear him. They would know that it wasn't just Fae he could exact his vengeance on—it was all beings. All would know the faces of his new Reapers. No more would they hide in the shadows.

No longer would the Reapers be legends. They would be flesh and bone, leaving others quaking, wondering who they'd come to slay.

Bran walked past the dead body of the woman of the house. There was still a smile on her face from the pleasure she received at Searlas's hand as he consumed her soul.

Her body needed to be removed. At least the husband's body was no longer on the stairs. It had been disposed of last night.

Bran was disappointed that the three children weren't at home, but all were off at university. That was too bad really. The two boys would make nice gifts for his army, but it was the girl he really wanted.

He walked up the stairs to the library and sat behind the desk. His gaze landed on the leather book he'd returned to the Fae Realm to acquire. The tome contained his lineage, but it wasn't his ancestors he was concerned with.

Opening the volume, he flipped through the pages until he found his name, as well as his wife's, and their children's. He leaned back in the chair and stared at the entries for a long time, trying to recall memories of his family. But there was nothing. Every happy thought had been sucked from him while he was in the Netherworld.

The facts were there, however. He knew he'd been married, and he knew his spouse's name. Bran also remembered he'd had children—both Fae and Halfling.

But that's all he recollected. He didn't remember holding his newborn babes, naming them, or even what their faces looked like. He wasn't sure if they were still alive, and honestly, he could care less.

They weren't his targets.

He followed the line of his children to their children and their children until he came to the last. The one thing he had that Death didn't was family, blood. They would make him strong.

So strong, that no matter what Erith did, she wouldn't be able to best him.

It was a blow she wouldn't see coming.

None of them would.

Death's Realm

Everything was changing. Erith could feel it in her bones. Her magic continued to fade rapidly, and it took everything she had to keep from showing it to her Reapers.

And Cael.

His eyes, however, saw everything. No matter what she did, he could see right through her. Only recently had he called her on it.

She'd believed all these years that he was afraid of her. When, in fact, he'd kept his silence out of respect. She knew that now because she recognized it in his silver eyes.

A sigh escaped her as she looked out her tower window to her realm. It had been her sanctuary, a place where she could be herself. Except, she was beginning to wonder if she'd built her own prison without even knowing it.

The sound of approaching footsteps caused her to turn her head to the side. Seamus halted at the doorway. She'd taken him as a prisoner after he helped Bran escape the Netherworld, and somehow, Seamus had become a friend of sorts.

"You should rest," he said.

She turned away from the window to face him but refused to

acknowledge his comment. "I gather your search has revealed nothing?"

He slapped his hand against his leg as his lips pulled down in a frown. "I'll not give up on figuring out how Bran is taking your magic."

"It may be out of your hands."

His black and silver brows knitted together in a deep frown. "It's gotten that bad, has it?"

"There is something I need to tell you."

"No," he said, shaking his head of black and silver hair as he took a step back. "Whatever you have to say, tell Cael."

She smiled gently. "I can't."

"Why not? He leads your Reapers."

How could she tell Seamus that she wanted Cael to remember her as she had been, not as what she was turning into? If she had to tell Cael what was coming, she'd never get it out.

And she wasn't entirely sure what Cael would do.

"I've given you refuge, Seamus," Erith said. "I could've killed you for what you did, but instead, I allowed you to make up for your transgression by helping me."

Seamus walked into the room until he stood before her. He looked at her with red eyes. "I'll be eternally grateful to you for that, but I'm begging you not to say whatever it is you want to tell me. It's bad news, and you want me to know, so I'll be the one to tell Cael. And that's because you don't expect to be around."

"That was a rather simple puzzle for you to figure out," she said with a smile.

He gave a bewildered shake of his head. "How can you smile?"

"Would you rather I cry. Scream?"

"I'd rather you fight!"

She walked to the bookshelf and ran her fingers along the spines of the books. "Do you know why I created the Reapers?"

"No," he said after a bit of hesitation.

Erith stopped at one of the books she'd seen Cael reading. Stroking the spine, she called up an image of the Reaper in her mind.

Strong. Confident. Clever.

And oh, so handsome.

"I was not born as you were," she explained and faced him. "I'm . . . more. When I fight, worlds tend to be destroyed. It's why I gave that job to the Reapers."

Seamus's lips pinched as he considered her words. "You mean, you destroy worlds like Rhi?"

"It's Rhi's anger which causes her to glow. When she loses control, she can blow up a realm. She can also create one. Mine isn't based on my emotions, but the physical act of battle itself."

"Are you related to Rhi?"

Erith felt her lips soften into a smile as she thought of the Light Fae. "That is a question for another day."

"You can still fight. Go to another realm and call for Bran. You know he'll meet you."

"It may come to that." But she feared it was already too late. Bran had taken much more of her magic—her very life force—than she allowed even Seamus to know.

Seamus ran a hand through his long, black hair liberally streaked with silver. "I know the Reapers would gladly fight and kill Bran themselves, but they can't even wound him now. Thankfully, he can't harm them either."

"So it falls to me," she finished.

"You can't let Bran win."

A butterfly soared through the open window and landed on the bookshelf near her. "I don't want that."

"You're afraid," he suddenly said.

She briefly closed her eyes before she looked at him. "I am Death for a reason, Seamus. Long before I was who you see now, I was wrath and hate. I lived for battle and the waste that followed wherever I went."

"What changed?"

Turning away before he saw the answer in her gaze, she said, "That is one secret I'll never share."

"You believe that you'll become that person again if you fight Bran."

"Yes. And I know I won't come back from it a second time."

Seamus walked to stand before her, making her meet his gaze. "No. I'm not going to sit around and watch you slowly weaken so Bran can kill you."

"It won't come to that."

The look of confusion fell away from Seamus's face. "Bran's taking more than your magic. I can't believe I didn't realize he was taking your life, as well."

"Cael splits his time between guarding the entrance to this realm and helping his men. He believes he can stop Bran if Bran happens to find my doorway, but Cael won't be able to do that."

Seamus's shoulders slumped, his gaze dropping to the floor.

Erith continued. "I don't want Cael seeing what I know is coming."

"If he calls for you and you don't go to him, he'll come here," Seamus said as he looked up at her.

She looked around the room. The tower had been her home for eons. Not once did she think she would be taken from it. "That is where you step in."

"You want me to try and stop Cael?" Seamus asked, his eyes wide with disbelief.

"Cael won't enter the tower without my permission. I'll remain inside, and when Cael comes, tell him I'm not here."

Seamus shook his head as he blew out a breath. "Forgive me for saying it, but you're mad if you think that'll work on him."

"It's why it's important that you make him believe it. I don't want him to see me. It'll shift his focus. And we both know he needs to be with his men."

"If there's anyone who should be by your side, it's Cael."

She cocked her head to the side. "Why do you say that?"

Seamus held her gaze for a full minute before he looked away. "Because he's the leader. And . . . well, I think he cares for you."

"Keep looking for ways to get to Bran. Cael and the others are going to need a way to kill him," she said before turning to leave.

"So you're just going to give up?" Seamus called after her.

Erith paused. Sometimes, without even trying, she could feel the weight of the sword in her palm. She wasn't sure what was worse—being killed by Bran, or returning to being Mistress of War.

If only there were a third option.

She continued on, not bothering to answer Seamus.

Ettie couldn't stop staring at herself in the bathroom mirror. The seconds she'd had in Daire's arms, his mouth on hers, replayed on a loop in her head.

She touched her lips and closed her eyes, recalling how his mouth moved over hers tenderly, seductively. All while his hand rested on her hip.

Just thinking of it caused her stomach to flip. She would still be in his arms if Bran hadn't arrived.

Just thinking of Bran made the image of Daire fade.

She opened her eyes as her hand dropped to the sink. Ettie still wasn't sure what to make of the fact that there were two Fae in her life. Daire's story was fantastic and terrifying. There was so much she wanted to ask him about the Fae, but it seemed trivial with what she and her sisters faced with Bran. Especially since they didn't know what Bran wanted.

Ettie wasn't going to let Bran anywhere near her sisters. She was prepared to do whatever it took to keep them safe. No sooner had the thought run through her mind than she realized that she couldn't watch over them all the time.

For all she knew, Fae from Bran's army had already approached her sisters. Surely, they would be cautious now. At least, she hoped they would.

Her chin dropped to her chest. There was no amount of warning, no training she could've done that would ever have prepared her for this. And to think she honestly believed she was ready for whatever came her way.

With her stomach churning, Ettie took deep, calming breaths. God, how silly Daire must think her. Their little session proved that no matter how quickly she moved, she was no match for him. To make matters worse, she knew he'd been holding back.

Bran wouldn't. He'd let loose with everything he had, and she'd be toast in a matter of seconds. Why had her father believed training her would be enough?

Her knowledge of fighting was enough to keep the arses away, but she'd be as insignificant as a gnat with the Fae. Running wasn't an option. So where did that leave her? Absolutely nowhere.

There was a soft rap on the door. Then Daire's voice came through the wood. "You'll have to come out sometime."

She pushed away from the sink and opened the door to face him. Daire was leaning a shoulder against the doorframe. His dark silver gaze captured hers.

"What is it?" he asked, concern deepening his voice.

She swallowed hard. "Do I have any chance of winning a battle against a Fae?"

"No."

It's what she expected, but to hear him say it aloud was like a sucker punch. She pushed past him and strode to the kitchen, but she halted when she realized she didn't know where to go or what to do.

"The only way you can harm a Fae is with a blade forged in the Fires of Erwar," Daire said as he came up behind her.

She slowly turned to face him. "Do you know where I can get one of those?"

"Have you trained with a sword?"

"Yes, but it's been several years."

He looked her up and down. "Which weapon do you prefer?"

"My staff."

His brows lifted in surprise. "Really?"

Her gaze lowered to his hand that he held out at his side. She blinked, and a spear was suddenly in his grasp. Her mouth fell open at the deep mahogany wood and the diamond shaped blade at the end that was easily a foot long.

"This should help," Daire said and handed it to her.

Her eyes snapped to his. "For me?"

"You can fight. All you need is a weapon."

She reached for it as he held it out to her. Her fingers brushed the wood, and the weapon disappeared.

"What the hell?" Daire murmured.

He called the weapon back, and again, as soon as she touched it, the spear vanished. They tried three more times, and the outcome was the same for each.

"I don't understand," Daire said.

Ettie's hopes were now dashed, but it wasn't Daire's fault. "Thank you for trying."

"Something is wrong," he said as if not hearing her. "I should be able to give you a weapon."

"Stop," she said when he began to try again. "Obviously, I'm not meant to have one."

Daire crossed his arms over his chest. "Then you're not getting anywhere near Bran again."

"If he wanted to kill me, wouldn't he have already done it?"

"I don't claim to know what's in that bastard's head. I wouldn't put anything past him."

Daire did have a point. Ettie's gaze lowered to his mouth. She really had to stop thinking about kissing him. There were much more important matters for her to concentrate on.

"Come here so I can kiss you again."

She felt her cheeks heat at having been caught staring. But she didn't look away. At his raised brow, she walked to him and rose up on her tiptoes to put her lips to his.

Strong arms came around her, pressing her against his hard body. She ran her hands over his thick shoulders and looped them around his neck. His head tilted to the side as his lips moved over hers.

Heat rushed through her, settling between her legs. The taste of him was exotic, erotic. Her entire body tingled with awareness.

And a deep-seated hunger.

Before she knew it, he lifted her, placing her on top of the table. The kiss deepened, sending sparks of need rushing through her. A thrilling and terrifying ravenous hunger consumed her. And with each kiss, Daire fed that craving.

Her legs wrapped around him as she surrendered to the yearning that beckoned her seductively. She shook with a desire that flared high and hot. All those nights with dreams of a lover stroking her body fell away as Daire surpassed them all.

He bent her back over his arm as his mouth trailed down her neck. She threaded her hands into his raven hair, the thick, cool strands sliding through her fingers.

She couldn't wait to feel him inside her. As if his thoughts were on the same thing, he rocked his arousal against her, making her moan.

Someone cleared their throat.

Ettie's stomach lurched as she jerked her head toward the door to find her sisters. She gaped at them, unsure of what to say or do. Daire lifted his head from between her breasts before slowly straightening.

"I knew we should've stayed away longer," Jamie said with a knowing grin as she elbowed Carrie.

Carrie was smiling from ear to ear. "Sorry to interrupt."

It was Daire who stepped away and held out his hand to her. Ettie took it and slid from the table to come to her feet. There wasn't an ounce of regret on Daire's face as he winked at her. She pointed to his hair since her fingers had messed it up. In response, he loosened the strap that held it and ran his hands through it.

And it made her melt.

"Yeah. We should've stayed away," Jamie mumbled.

Ettie inwardly shook herself and faced her sisters. "It's fine. Come inside out of the cold."

Carrie sauntered in and set the groceries on the table. As she took each item out of the bag, she began talking to Daire. Ettie didn't hear a word of it. Her ears were still ringing with the sounds of Daire's groans.

"I'm happy for you."

She swung her head to look at Jamie beside her. Ettie glanced at Daire and saw his gaze on her. They exchanged a smile before she returned her regard to Jamie. "It's nothing."

"That definitely looked like something," her middle sister said with a grin, her blue eyes alight. "And might I say, it's about damn time."

That made Ettie laugh out loud.

The resulting quiet had her glancing around the kitchen to Carrie, who stared wide-eyed at her. Ettie then turned her gaze to Daire. His silver eyes said one thing: he wanted her.

Jamie chuckled. "I think you've shocked Carrie. Though it has been a while since you've laughed."

"No. That's not right," Ettie argued.

Jamie lifted her brows. "Tell me when you laughed last."

"Well. . . ." But as she went through her memories, Ettie realized it had been a while. She smiled, but that was usually the extent of it.

"See?" Jamie replied with a nod, proving her point.

Ettie bit her lip. "Have I been that uptight?"

"Oh, yeah. Then again, you do shoulder most of the burdens," Carrie said.

She met her sister's blue gaze. "I do."

"That's going to change," Jamie stated.

"We'll worry about that after this Bran thing is finished."

Carrie made a gagging sound. "Did you have to mention him?"

"He came by after you two left," Daire stated.

For the next thirty minutes, Ettie and Daire told them what had happened when Bran visited. The talk then turned to different ways to keep him away while Carrie began cooking.

The conversation lasted well after dinner, yet nothing was resolved. But then again, Ettie hadn't expected a miracle. It was enough that they had Daire there to help.

After she'd finished the last of the dishes, Ettie wiped her hands as she looked to the living room where Daire was engrossed in conversation with her sisters. She grabbed her coat and walked outside, needing some fresh air. She made her way to the stream to listen to the water and look up at the stars.

The crunch of shoes on the grass let her know someone was

approaching. She looked over her shoulder and felt a little thrill run through her when she spotted Daire.

"You can't hurt Bran," she said.

Daire stopped beside her and shook his head. "Unfortunately, I can't. I can kill those in his army, but they'll rise again."

"Oh, joy. That makes me feel better."

He faced her and put a finger beneath her chin to turn her head to him. "It doesn't matter if Bran comes to kill you or to take something from you. You're not in this fight alone. I'm with you. As the other Reapers will be."

"I thank you for that. I'm worried about my sisters."

"Right now, Bran's attention is on you. I wish I knew why, but perhaps we should be thankful that Jamie and Carrie haven't drawn his gaze too much."

She drew in a deep breath of the cold, damp air. "I saw you looking at the locked cabinet at dinner."

"I was."

"It's been passed down through each generation," she said as she turned to face him. "My father handed me the key the night he died."

Daire watched her for a moment. "It holds things about the Fae, doesn't it?"

"A few books my ancestors discovered. Mostly, there are journals written by those in my family who have gone in search of the Fae."

"Search? Ettie, the Fae have chosen Ireland as their home. Fae are everywhere. Well, except Killarney. But you can walk in any city and be surrounded by them."

She laughed despite the tears gathering in her eyes. "Why didn't anyone in my family see them?"

"I don't know. It's odd that you'd know of your heritage yet not have seen a Fae."

She sniffed, wondering the same thing as she fought the tears for herself and her father. "So if I went to Dublin, I'd see Fae?"

"Everywhere. Some use glamour, but many don't bother."

"Papa's great search was for the Light Castle."

Daire moved closer and put his hands on her waist. "Shall I take you there?"

"You'd do that?"

He nodded, smiling. "Though I doubt it's what you think it is."

"Is it beautiful?"

"Very."

"Then it's what I think it is."

He linked his hands at her back. "Then I shall take you. I don't think a Halfling has ever walked those halls, but I know someone who'll stand with you."

"Who?" she asked.

"An infamous Fae who likes to buck the rules. I mentioned her before. Her name is Rhi."

CHAPTER
twelve

Not once did Daire consider that he should hold back his desire for Ettie. It felt too good to have her in his arms and to taste those amazing lips of hers. He wasn't going to pass up the chance for more.

And more of her.

"What are you thinking when you look at me that way?" she asked in a breathless whisper.

Oh, the things he wanted to tell her. Like that he would make her scream in pleasure and beg for more. Ettie had been closed off from the world. It was time to release her from her self-imposed prison.

He leaned down until his lips hovered over her neck just below her ear. "I'm thinking of all the ways I'd like to tear off your clothes so I can have you bared before me. I want to see you beneath the sun and the moon, so I can kiss, lick, and touch every inch of you."

Her breathing quickened as she leaned her head to the side, exposing her neck to him. "Yes," she murmured.

"I want to show you what it means to be held in the arms of someone who yearns to worship your body. I want you all to myself with no outside distractions. I want to fill you, to join our bodies and make love to you for centuries."

She turned her face to his and kissed him as if there were no tomorrow, as if she were drowning in desire, and he was the only thing that could save her.

He returned her kiss, their need erupting with such force that nothing could've pulled them apart. They were past the point of stopping. But Daire was cognizant enough to realize he couldn't take Ettie beneath the stars on her land because Bran might see them.

Daire ended the kiss and held her face between her hands. He looked into her eyes. "I want you. But not here."

"I don't care where we go, as long as you don't stop kissing or touching me."

That's all the permission he needed. Daire teleported them to a deserted isle near Greece. Her gaze widened before a smile pulled at her lips.

"Where are we?" she asked while shrugging out of her coat.

"Greece."

She yanked open his flannel. "That's nice."

He chuckled before taking her lips again.

She pushed him back and put a finger to his mouth. "I'm going to remove your clothes, and I can't do that with you kissing me."

Daire snapped his fingers, and his clothes disappeared. Her mouth fell open while her eyes raked down his body. His desire skyrocketed as he watched her reaction to seeing him.

"Dear God," she whispered and spread her hands over his chest. "You're magnificent. All these muscles."

He held still—barely—when she caressed down his chest to his stomach and back up to his arms and shoulders. Then her gaze dropped to his cock.

His arousal jumped at her perusal. But it was her long fingers wrapping around him that nearly made his knees buckle.

"Perfection," she said.

Her hand moved up and down his length, ratcheting his desire to the point he was fast losing control.

"If you don't kiss me right now, I think I might die," Ettie said.

He slid his hand around the back of her head and pulled her to him, plundering her lips so she'd know just how much he craved her, how much he burned for her.

He called a blanket to him, spreading it on the ground beside them with his magic. Daire backed her onto it before making her clothes vanish.

She sucked in a breath as the sea breeze moved over her. He looked down at her and stroked her face. This was their night. It might be their only one, and he wasn't going to let anything get in the way.

"Let me look at you," he bade.

Lips swollen from his kisses curved into a grin as she stepped out of his arms. Daire's mouth went dry when he drank in her beauty.

She had small, firm breasts with pink nipples that his mouth ached to tease. His gaze followed the indent of her waist to her hips and the triangle of blond curls at the juncture of her thighs.

If he thought her legs were amazing in denim, it was nothing compared to seeing those long limbs bared and waiting for his hands to caress them.

"Beautiful," he said when he met her gaze.

She held out her hand. He grasped it and closed the short distance between them until their bodies were skin-to-skin. His arms wrapped around her as he looked down at her.

"I don't think I can wait another second," she told him.

He rubbed his nose against hers. "We've got all night."

"Then take me now. We can go slow later."

As if he needed to be told twice.

In the next second, Daire had them lying on the blanket. He ran his hands along her body, loving the feel of her skin. But she rolled him onto his back and straddled him.

He gazed up at her in wonder and delight. The moon cast a bluish light over her body, giving her an otherworldly look. But it was the desire in her eyes and the way she embraced her yearning and the needs of her body that showed her Fae heritage.

A moan rumbled in his chest when she took his cock in hand and brought him to her entrance. He was about to mention protection, but his mind went blank when she lowered herself onto his length. The moment he felt her wetness, he almost came.

She was tight and hot. He gripped her hips as she continued to lower herself down upon him. When she was fully seated, she dropped her head back, causing her breasts to thrust forward.

He might not have gotten to tease the folds of her sex or bring her to the edge of release by licking her clit. But he would have a taste of her breasts.

Daire sat up and wrapped his lips around one turgid peak. A tremor went through her back as her arms locked about him. He lightly scraped her nipples with his teeth before flicking his tongue back and forth rapidly. Then he suckled deeply.

Her hips began to rock. The more attention he gave her, the

faster she moved. His mouth switched to her other breast and began all over again.

With her nails digging into the back of his neck, he recognized that she needed more. He flipped them so she was on her back. Then he pulled out and thrust hard, filling her until he touched her womb.

Her back arched as a pleasure-filled cry rent the air. He held still, letting her feel him completely before he slowly withdrew.

He looked between them to her opening that glistening beneath the moonlight, he wanted to give her a night she'd never forget. And one he wouldn't either.

"Please," she said as her hands fisted the blanket.

Daire ran his hands along her inner thighs. Her greedy body wanted release, and he desperately wanted to give it to her. After a bit of teasing.

He circled her swollen clit with his finger, which caused her eyes to fly open. Her mouth opened, but no words came out as he began to thrum the small bud.

"I'm going to fill you again," he told her while continuing to stroke her. "Your orgasm will make you mindless. But first, I'm going to make you climax with my fingers and mouth."

She nodded as her chest rose and fell rapidly. Her hips rose as she moaned loudly. It wasn't long before her eyes closed and her head began thrashing side to side.

While continuing to thumb her clit, he thrust two fingers of his other hand slowly inside her. She cried out his name, her hips bucking for more.

Soon, her cries filled the air as he brought her closer and closer to her climax. He began moving his fingers faster. Then he bent and lapped at her clit with his tongue.

That's all it took for her body to jerk as the orgasm swept

through her. He watched the ecstasy cross her face while her body clamped around his fingers, but this was just the beginning of their night.

He withdrew his hand and brought his cock to her entrance once more. With the climax still pulsing, he shoved inside her. That wrenched another cry of pleasure from her.

He wasn't going to allow the orgasm to end softly. Instead, he began driving inside her with the hard, deep thrusts she'd begged for earlier.

Her legs locked around him while her hips rose up to meet him. He braced his hands on either side of her head and found himself gazing deep into her blue eyes.

The need he saw within them shifted and changed into something deeper, more profound. There was no time to wonder about it with the rapture that was overtaking them.

The breeze cooled their sweat-soaked bodies as they continued their dance, drawing ever closer to the edge of bliss. An animalistic frenzy engulfed Daire. He neither understood it nor wanted to stop it.

Because he had Ettie in his arms, claiming her as his.

Her lips formed a silent O. It was the subtle stiffening of her body that let him know she was about to peak. He moved faster, drove inside her harder until he felt her walls clamp down around him.

She screamed his name as her body jerked with the force of the orgasm. He never stopped moving, continued to pound into her until he felt his own climax.

There was no stopping it once it had begun. He gave a final thrust and held still. As his seed filled her, he realized this was the first time he'd ever had sex with a human or a Halfling. And he wondered if he'd gotten her with child.

That thought should've scared him, but it didn't. He didn't want children, but he did want Ettie and everything that came with her.

He looked down at her as she lay there with her eyes closed. She was the most beautiful thing he'd ever seen. It made him wonder how he could've ever imagined himself with anyone else. Ettie was . . . special.

"Can we do that again?" She smiled and slowly opened her eyes.

"I'll happily make love to you for as long as you let me."

"I like the sound of that."

He pulled out of her and rolled to the side. She moved with him, resting her head on his chest. Daire looked up at the stars and smiled.

"You're smiling," Ettie said.

Chuckling, he glanced at her. "You did that."

"You know exactly what to say."

"It's the truth."

She idly ran her fingers over his chest. "I wish we could remain like this."

And just like that, Bran and the war intruded. The smile melted from Daire's face. He wasn't angry with her for bringing it up. It was a fact neither of them could escape.

"How long can we stay here?" she asked.

He put his free arm behind his head. "A little longer."

"I shouldn't have brought it up."

"It's fine," he told her and kissed the top of her head. "We'll return to the cottage, and I'll call the other Reapers in. We'll figure out a way to stop Bran."

She blew out a soft breath. "I could be an asset if only I could touch a Fae weapon. Does that happen to other Halflings?"

"No. There has to be a reason for it, and we'll get to the bottom of that, as well."

"You're so confident," she said as she tilted her face to him.

He smiled at her. "I'm a Reaper."

"You say that as if it says it all."

"It does. I was always reckless, but I was good in battle."

Ettie licked her lips. "You said Death chose each Fae because of their skill, but also because they were betrayed before they were killed."

"Yes. I was betrayed by a group of friends."

CHAPTER

thirteen

A betrayal, no matter by who, was one that cut deeply and left a scar that never fully healed.

Ettie's heart broke for Daire and the way he casually said those words. He spoke them as if they no longer wounded him, but she wasn't sure that was the case.

She raised her head to look at him. Clear, silver eyes met hers. She ran her fingers through his hair, starting at his forehead and combing back.

"Don't be sad for me," he said.

"How can you ask that? You were betrayed by friends."

He wrinkled his nose. "I use that term loosely to describe those individuals. You see, I was known for being wild and irresponsible. I was careless and hasty and often reacted without thinking things through. A classic case of recklessness."

She propped up on her elbow and rested her chin on her hand. "You liked trouble."

"Not really. But it always seemed to find me. It wasn't until I was dying that I realized I constantly found myself in difficult situations because of my decisions and the crowd I hung with."

"You talk as if you blame yourself for your betrayal."

He shrugged, a crooked smile tilting his lips. "In a way, I do. All the signs were there, telling me what was coming, but I didn't heed them."

"What happened?"

His gaze slid back to the heavens. "I hated conformity of any kind. If there was a rule, I was going to break it."

"That isn't true. You didn't turn Dark."

There was a slight grin upon his lips when he glanced at her. "True, but I imagine my father would argue with you. My mother abandoned us after my youngest brother was born. She left my dad to raise five boys on his own. I was the middle, and pretty much left to my own devices. The older I got, my father tried to get me to take more responsibility, but I refused. And my two younger siblings followed my example."

Ettie inwardly winced. She could only imagine what Daire's dad had gone through being left by the woman he loved and then having to go on with life while raising five boys.

"My situation wasn't as bad. My mother died instead of leaving, but it did a number on my father," she said. "I often heard him crying late at night when he thought we were asleep."

Daire ran his fingers up and down her back. "Mine refused to talk about my mother. He never stopped us from talking about her, but he wouldn't speak her name. He shut down those emotions."

"He likely had to in order to raise all of you."

"Yeah," Daire murmured. "I think he did. And I didn't help matters. It got to the point that he told me to either straighten up or he was kicking me out."

She bit her lip and scrunched up her face.

Daire turned his head to her. "I left without a backward glance. After six months with the group of Fae I was with, I realized I wanted to go home. They were doing things that were coming closer and closer to the side of the Dark, and it wasn't a place I wanted to be."

"What did you do?"

"I distanced myself from them."

She raised her brows. "That's great."

"Not completely, though I didn't realize it until it was too late. You see, when I left them, they brought in my younger brothers."

"Oh."

"They thought recruiting my siblings would get me back. What it did was piss me off. I went to my brothers and told them what would happen if they stayed with the group. One returned home, but the youngest remained."

Ettie pushed up on her hand to look down at him. "At least you got one to realize what those Fae were."

"It would've been better if I hadn't. The gang threatened my youngest brother, so I went after them. I fought many, but in the end, I realized it was a trap. But it was too late. My brother had returned to our family without me knowing it. The group wanted me."

"How many stood against you?"

"Ten. I killed four before they got me." He looked back to the stars. "As I lay dying, they told me how they had killed my brothers and father. My family was dead. Because of me."

She leaned down and placed her lips on his for a soft kiss. "I'm so sorry."

His arms came around her tightly. They remained that way for a long time before he let out a shuddering breath. "My first assignment as a Reaper was to help Cael and Eoghan execute the rest of the gang."

"Good," she said. "You had closure. Everyone needs that."

"Even you."

She leaned up, her arms braced against his chest. "What do you mean?"

"Your question when we first met."

"Ah." She sat up and tucked her legs against her while still leaning on him. "I don't think it's something I'll ever know, and I'm not sure it matters anymore."

He quirked a black brow, one side of his mouth curving into a smile. "Really?"

"Okay. So maybe that's a tiny lie," she admitted with a laugh. "After all you've told me about the Fae, I don't understand why we've never seen one before you and Bran."

"It's odd, I'll grant you that. I walked Killarney twice while veiled and didn't spot one Fae besides Bran."

She drummed her fingers on his chest. "Do you think there's something about the town that keeps others away?"

"It didn't keep Bran or me from coming here. Yet, there's no doubt the Fae know something we don't. I think it's time to find out what that is, though you might be better off without the Fae."

She looked across the moon-drenched waters to the lights on the mainland of Greece. "Or we find out the reason so other cities can implement the same thing. Whether it works on Reapers or not, it seems to on the regular Fae."

"I agree. We'll look into it as soon as Bran's taken care of."

Ettie couldn't help but grin as he included her in on the plans. It felt amazing to be a part of something as grand as the Reapers. Perhaps it was a bit naïve of her, but she wasn't afraid of Bran with Daire there.

Of course, part of that might be the fact that she was still glowing from their lovemaking.

"Do you really believe we can beat Bran?"

Daire nodded. "Of course, because to even consider the alternative is to allow him a victory in the first step to defeating us. I refuse to give him that."

"The locked cabinet you asked about, I want to show you what's inside," she said.

"All right."

"I don't know why it's locked. It always has been, though."

He smoothed a lock of her hair out of her eyes and tucked it behind her ear, holding it there when the breeze threatened to yank it away. "Usually, there's something important when someone puts a lock on something."

"I've looked at everything inside."

"It could be that you didn't know what you were looking at."

She had to admit that was a possibility. "That's why you need to have a look for yourself."

"You make it sound as if you want to do it now."

"I don't, but I'm afraid to wait."

He brought her head down to kiss her deeply. When she leaned back, her clothes were back in place, as were his. Daire then sat up and took her hand, bringing her up with him when he stood.

"Ready?"

"Only if you promise to bring me back here."

He yanked her against him and held her with one arm. "You have my word."

She held his gaze as Greece fell away and her home came into view. After only a few seconds, she regretted leaving Greece. There, it had only been the two of them, and if she didn't have her sisters to worry about, she might have remained. But the right thing to do was to return.

They walked to the cottage and then went inside. Carrie was taking a bath, while Jamie was on the phone with her beau. Ettie left Daire by the cabinet while she got the key.

She sat after she'd unlocked it and opened the doors. One by one, she pulled out the books and journals and handed them to Daire to inspect. He carefully looked through each one before moving on to the next.

They were there for over two hours before her sisters joined them. The four of them sat in a semi-circle, their gazes locked on Daire.

He found very few things in the journals that were of interest. Ettie was shocked to learn that most of what was inside them was erroneous findings about the Fae. And, for some reason, she thought about the journal her father gave her when she turned sixteen. She hadn't written one word in it, but perhaps now it was time for that to change.

The only thing left in the cabinet was a jar of what looked like dirt.

"Yuck," Carrie said. "We should throw that out."

But Daire shook his head. "Not until we know what it is."

"You said yourself, most of the stuff in the journals is wrong," Jamie said. "That's probably just regular dirt."

Ettie, however, agreed with Daire. "Better safe than sorry."

When Daire kept looking at the dirt, Jamie and Carrie left and went to their rooms since there was nothing else. Ettie watched the frown on his face deepen.

"What is it?" she asked.

"I don't know. I can feel some magic in it."

Now that surprised her. "Really?"

"It's faint, but it's there."

"In dirt?"

He shoved his black locks out of his face and looked at her. "It's true this dirt could be from your land, but the fact that it has magic within it is intriguing. I want to learn where it came from."

"I want to know why we have it. Papa never mentioned it. It's like he forgot it was even in there."

"I didn't see it until you brought it out," Daire confessed.

Now, wasn't that weird.

She took the jar and tilted it this way and that as she looked at the dark granules within. It even still looked moist, as if it hadn't been in there for who knew how long. If her father had brought it, he would've spoken to her about it.

That meant the dirt was even older than she'd first thought. It could've come from her grandfather or even her great-grandfather.

There were so many questions running through her mind about a simple jar of dirt. Then, she calmly returned it to the cabinet, because in the back of her mind, she somehow knew it wasn't time for her to learn those answers yet.

Daire helped her replace all the journals and books. She relocked the cabinet out of habit and got to her feet. Daire stood and took her hand as they walked to her room.

He stood in the doorway as she put the key away beneath her socks. She closed the drawer and looked at him. They stared at each other for several quiet minutes before he pushed away from the doorway and moved to her.

"Will you stay?" she asked.

"Yes."

There was a smile on her face and in her heart as she

undressed and put on her pajamas. He was already in the bed when she lifted the covers and slid in beside him.

He pulled her down onto his chest and kissed her forehead. "Get some sleep. I'll be here."

She took a deep breath and closed her eyes, giving in to the slumber quickly wrapping her in its embrace.

There were defining moments in everyone's life. One of those was when Daire made love to Ettie. He'd known it as soon as he tasted her kiss, but once their bodies were joined, the moment became etched in his mind.

He remained near all night. Most of it was by her side, but he also patrolled the O'Byrne property as well as sent out a call to the Reapers.

His gaze moved to the window as the first rays of the new day filtered through the window and into the bedroom. He followed the beams as they ran over the floor to the bed and across his legs to Ettie's.

He couldn't help but smile at her while she lay on her back, her face turned to him, and her arm stretched out beside her. But that smile died when he saw the sword in her hand.

The long, slightly curved, black blade sparkled in the sunlight. The longer he looked at it, the more he knew it was Fae.

Ettie took a deep breath and opened her eyes. As soon as she did, the sword vanished. Daire didn't move, he didn't even breathe.

"Good morning," she mumbled and turned to snuggle against him.

"Morning." He held her, his gaze still locked on the spot on the bed where the sword had been.

What the hell was going on? There was no way Ettie had been faking her distress about not having a weapon to fight Bran. That meant she had no idea about the black blade.

And he wasn't sure he should tell her.

"We should get up soon," he said. "The other Reapers will be here shortly."

After a big yawn, she rolled out of bed and shuffled into the bathroom. Daire sat up and said, "Cael."

He knew Cael would hear him and come immediately. Daire rose and walked into the kitchen to find the leader of the Reapers at the table eating one of Carrie's scones.

"How long have you been here?" Daire asked.

"About five minutes," Cael said before popping the last of the treat into his mouth.

Daire looked over his shoulder at the bathroom door that was closed. The shower was running, but Carrie and Jamie were also moving about in their rooms.

"Daire?" Cael said as he got to his feet.

His head swung back to Cael. "Have you ever heard of a black Fae blade?"

"Why do you ask?"

Daire noticed that Cael hadn't exactly answered his question. "Ettie has trained her entire life for battle. She's quick and very good, but she didn't have a weapon. I tried to give her one yesterday, but every time she touched it, it disappeared."

"That doesn't make sense."

"I didn't think so either. I was going to have you give her one to see if it happened again."

Cael crossed his arms over his chest. "What does this have to do with a black blade?"

"She was holding a sword of solid black as she slept, but when she woke, it disappeared. It was Fae. I'm sure of it."

At that moment, Carrie's door opened, and she walked out dressed for the day, only to stumble to a halt when she spotted Cael. In the blink of an eye, she changed from a sweet girl into a sexy woman.

"Who's this, Daire?" she said as she walked up, all smiles.

Daire gave a shake of his head in frustration. "Carrie, this is Cael, the leader of the Reapers. Cael, Carrie."

Cael dropped his arms to his sides and bowed his head to her. "Hello."

"If I'd known we'd have such a hunk in the kitchen, I would've gotten up earlier," she said, batting her lashes at Cael.

Her gaze fell to the plate of scones before swinging back to Cael. She then walked to him and reached up, wiping the corner of his mouth where a crumb was.

"Did you like my scones?" she asked in a husky whisper.

Unperturbed, Cael smiled. "Very much."

"Shall I cook you something?"

"Perhaps later."

Daire stepped in before Carrie could go on. "Tell Ettie we'll be at the top of the mountain."

With a look at Cael, Daire teleported to the peak where he'd first shown himself to Ettie. Cael was right behind him, and then Kyran, Talin, Neve, Fintan, and Baylon appeared.

"A black blade," Fintan said.

Daire couldn't believe he was so wrapped up with Ettie and the weapon that he hadn't realized the others had been veiled inside the house, as well. It was a good way to get himself—and everyone—killed.

"I've never heard of such a weapon," Baylon said.

Neve shook her head. "Me either."

Daire raked a hand through his hair and looked at the ground. "Forget the weapon for now. We need to discuss Bran. I don't think he suspects we're here, but just in case, we should spread out and be prepared for him to test the area for us. He's already done that with me."

"How did he miss you?" Talin asked.

Daire shrugged. "I stood behind Ettie."

"Smart," Kyran said.

Cael hadn't spoken since the cottage. His gaze also hadn't moved from Daire. "We're taking a chance that Bran is focusing on this family and not his other descendants."

"He's here, though," Neve said.

Daire shrugged. "That could be to throw us off."

"But you don't think so," Kyran said.

Daire gave a shake of his head as he looked down at the cottage to see Ettie walk out and look their way. "Bran is intent on having Ettie. I thought it was something about the land because he asked her if she inherited it. She lied to him." Daire looked at the others. "Other than Bran and us, there are no Fae in the area. The O'Byrne family has never encountered one before. They've been searching for Fae all these years."

"That's vexing," Talin mumbled, a frown furrowing his brow.

"It's fekking odd," Fintan stated.

Daire squeezed the bridge of his nose with his thumb and forefinger. "There is a locked cabinet within the cottage. The sisters opened it for me last night. It's filled with books and journals where every one of the girls' ancestors got it wrong about the Fae. But, it was an old jar of dirt that Ettie pulled out, which I didn't see until she handed it to me that's the most troubling."

"Why?" Cael asked.

"I sensed magic in it. It was faint."

Baylon rubbed a hand over his jaw. "All of this is weird."

A flash of the black sword filled Daire's mind. "Then there's the weapon."

"I think there's more to these O'Byrne women than we realize," Cael said.

Neve fingered one of the many knives on her person. "It could be why Bran is interested in them."

"Her," Daire corrected. "He's shown no interest in Jamie or Carrie. Only Ettie."

Fintan moved to the start of the path leading down to the cottage. "We've set up a perimeter. If anyone crosses it or teleports in, we'll know."

One by one, his brethren began walking down the path, leaving Daire with Cael.

"Our perimeter is strong enough that we'll be alerted even if Death pays us a visit," Cael said.

Daire nodded to let Cael know he'd heard him. It was the knot of apprehension in Daire's gut that made him wary of everything.

He turned his head to Cael. "You know what the black sword is, don't you?"

Cael sighed and looked out over the valley below them. "There are many things we witness, hear, and read in our lives before and after we become Reapers."

"True."

"I don't know facts, Daire. I want you to understand that. It's something I read once a very long time ago when I was only a lad. It was a story about a god of war, though some said it was really a goddess. This being was war. The pictures drawn with the story showed a black sword."

Daire knew all stories were based on fact. His head snapped toward Ettie. "You can't think she's related to this god or goddess."

"Guessing will get us nowhere. But there is someone who would know."

"Death," Daire said.

Cael moved to stand beside him. "I'm not saying she'll tell us anything, but we can ask. The quicker we learn the reason Bran wants Ettie, the sooner we can stop his attack."

"I don't think we have long."

"I know we don't," Cael said.

Daire glanced at him. "I . . . ah . . . I slept with her."

"I know."

Two words. That was all. Daire didn't know what he'd expected, but he was glad Cael knew. The one thing Daire hated was secrets.

"I'm going to Erith," Cael said.

When Daire looked over, Cael was gone. He blew out a breath and started down the mountain, eager to be near Ettie again.

Cael knew he was pushing his luck by visiting Death again so soon, but he had a good reason. Never mind that he was glad he had motivation because he'd been searching for some.

His concern for Erith grew with every heartbeat, but he wouldn't let anyone know just how worried he'd become. Or how she occupied his thoughts—both waking and dreaming.

He stepped through the Fae doorway on the small isle and immediately relaxed. There was something about Death's realm that always comforted him. Probably because she was there.

With no time to lose, he started toward the tower. As he walked the meandering path, he expected to see her with every turn. She always knew when he arrived and was there, waiting.

Except he reached the tower without a single glimpse of her. And his worry skyrocketed.

"Cael."

He spun around at the sound of Seamus's voice. The Dark Fae made his way to Cael from the dense forest. Cael looked behind Seamus. "Where's Erith?"

"She's not here."

Seamus was lying. Cael didn't know how he knew, he just did. And there was only one reason Seamus would lie to him—Erith had asked him to.

That stung far more than Cael expected. He took a step back as if physically hit. Though he wanted to shout and demand Death show herself, he didn't. Nor did he look up at the tower to see if she was at one of the many windows.

"She's gone and didn't tell me where," Seamus said as he stopped at the table and chairs and lowered himself into one of the seats.

If this were the game they wanted to play, then Cael would go along with it. For now. "What has your research revealed?"

"Unfortunately, not much."

"So you still don't know how Bran is stealing her magic?"

Seamus stilled, his gaze snapping to Cael's face. "Whether you believe it or not, I'm loyal to her. As strong and powerful as Erith is, she underestimated Bran, but that doesn't mean I'm going to stop looking. There is something, somewhere in those books of hers, and I'll find it."

"Before it's too late?"

The Fae studied him a long moment. "If it's within my power, yes. You and your Reapers need to step up your game and help."

"I won't fail her."

"She knows that," Seamus said softly.

Cael took a deep breath and looked at the forest that surrounded the entire realm. "Have you ever heard of a black Fae blade?"

"Black, you say?" Seamus asked as he sat forward, resting his arms on the iron table.

Cael turned his head back to the Fae. "Yes."

"Nothing definitive. Just a legend about a being of w—"

It was the way Seamus's eyes briefly grew round that told Cael the bastard knew something.

Seamus quickly recovered and cleared his throat. "Excuse me. As I was saying, a being of war."

Cael walked until he stood so close to Seamus that the Fae had to lean his head back to look at Cael. "Tell her I was here. And if either of you has information on this blade, we need it. It could be what ultimately ends Bran."

With that, he spun on his heel and stalked away. As he did, the hairs on the back of his neck rose. He was being watched. And he knew by who—Death.

fifteen

The arrival of so many Fae on the property affected each of the O'Byrne sisters. But it was more than that. It was the restlessness, the tension, and the unease that grew like silent, grotesque entities all around them.

And there was nothing Ettie could do about it.

She'd believed she would feel better with the Reapers there. But that's not what happened. She stood outside, looking at the mountains. The Reapers were veiled, so she never knew exactly where they were, but it didn't stop her nervousness.

Or maybe it was the thought of the upcoming battle that made her jump at every sound.

It didn't matter how much training she had, nothing could prepare her for an actual battle. And that's exactly what was coming. Worse, it was a clash involving magic.

Her gaze turned to the garage where Jamie had the bonnet of the car raised as she leaned over it, looking at the engine. It had been ten minutes since Jamie moved. She held a tool in hand, but her mind was elsewhere.

Ettie swiveled her head to the other side and looked through the window at Carrie. Her sister had been cooking nonstop. It was what she did when she was anxious.

The calm Ettie had always relied upon at the cottage was shattered. She didn't blame Daire or the Reapers. The fault lay with Bran.

Ettie raised her hands and turned them palm up as she looked at them. Bran was coming for her. It didn't matter why, only that she was able to ready herself.

But how did one prepare for such an event? She would fight. It wasn't in her to stand meekly by as Bran said or did whatever he intended. It was in her bones, in her very spirit to stand for what she believed in, to defend her family, her home, and herself.

She hadn't been raised to be a lady. She'd been raised to be a warrior. Her father had warned her to be ready, and though she didn't know if Bran was what he'd meant, it really didn't matter.

Because she was ready.

Whether she had a Fae weapon or not, she would fight. She might die within the first few seconds of battle, but at least her sisters would see that she'd tried, that she'd given it her all.

A cold chill slithered down her spine in warning. She dropped her arms and slowly lifted her head. Then she turned and came face-to-face with Bran.

"Ah, I thought so," he said pensively.

She wasn't worried about Bran's arrival. The Reapers were there, but that didn't stop the flutter of fear and dread. So she raised a brow. "What are you talking about?"

"How long have you known who I was?"

Ettie briefly thought about lying, but what was the point? "A few days. You were too . . . aggressive in your approach."

He gave her a flat look. "You were dying for male attention. It wouldn't have mattered what I looked like. You would've still acted the same."

Out of the corner of her eye, she saw Jamie take notice of them and straighten. Ettie didn't look her way or to the cottage. Bran's attention needed to be all on her, not her sisters.

"Maybe. Maybe not. The fact is, you screwed up," Ettie said. "You were too concerned with my sisters liking you and learning if this land was mine when you should've been trying to sleep with me."

"If I wanted you in my bed, you would've been there."

His retort didn't hurt her as it might have weeks earlier. "What do you want?"

"You know."

She widened her eyes and shrugged her shoulders. "If I did, I wouldn't have asked."

"I believe you. Because if you knew, you wouldn't speak with such insolence."

"Then tell me."

His gaze narrowed as he gradually began to smile. "I don't think so. I rather enjoy the thought of you fretting over something you can neither change nor stop."

Ettie fought not to say Daire's name. Why weren't the Reapers attacking? What were they waiting for? She didn't care what Bran wanted. She only needed him gone. Forever.

Bran chuckled and shook his head. "It's sad, really."

"What?" She couldn't seem to help herself. Even though she knew he was egging her on and she should keep her mouth shut, she kept the conversation going.

"You sided with the wrong people. The Reapers can't help you."

Her stomach fell to her feet like lead. How had he guessed?

Bran's smile was gone as he took a step toward her, his face lined with anger. "We've clashed so many times. I know their methods. Just as they know they can't hurt me. It's why they've not attacked. That is what you've been waiting on, isn't it?"

She didn't think it was possible to feel such hate for someone, but Ettie was literally shaking with fury. She refused to confirm or deny anything. "Leave."

"I'll decide when I'm done with you."

"No."

A muscle ticked in his jaw. "Perhaps I should demonstrate just how powerful I am."

He snapped his fingers, an evil smile in place. Then he pointed toward the house. Ettie looked at Carrie and found a tall Fae with blazing red eyes behind her sister.

"Carrie!" Ettie shouted.

But it was too late. Just like that, the Fae took her sister.

Ettie swung around to Jamie in time to see Jamie slam the bonnet down on the hands of a Fae before turning and grabbing one of their training staffs.

A smile grew on Ettie's face as she watched Jamie fight, but it was short-lived. The Fae threw what looked like a bubble toward the staff, and it disintegrated the weapon immediately.

And then Jamie was gone, too.

Ettie fisted her hands at her sides. Where the hell were Daire and the Reapers?

"Was it Cael who promised to protect you?" Bran asked. "Which Reaper assured you they could safeguard you from me?"

She glared at him, despising him with everything she was. "No one told me anything. I figured out you were Fae all on my one. So go feck yourself."

"The Reapers can't stand against me. They know they can't win either. I will kill each and every one of them. You need to understand you're on your own. Because where are they now?" he asked with his arms wide as he looked around.

She didn't want to talk about the Reapers. Not now. "Where are my sisters?"

"I'll be holding them." Bran dropped his arms and smiled at her. "They'll be returned as soon as you give me what I want."

"I can't until you tell me what it is."

"You'll sign over this land and your home as well as all of your belongings to me."

Of all the things she'd thought he might want, that was a strange request. "And if I don't?"

"You'll never see your sisters again."

The full comprehension that she was well and truly alone in this was like having a boulder dropped on her. She wanted to cry and scream and hit something—namely, Bran.

Daire wasn't there for her to turn to and ask for guidance. He claimed to know Bran, and that could've been an asset. If Bran had actually been there for her. Now, however, she'd have to go with her gut.

She was sick to her stomach at the knowledge that she had trusted Bran and the Reapers. And for what? When she needed them, they hadn't helped her. Her sisters were now under Bran's control, which meant that Ettie would do whatever he wanted.

"If I do this, my sisters will be returned, unharmed?" she asked.

Bran wrinkled his face, his lips twisting. "Relatively unharmed."

"If anyone touches them with or without magic, this deal is off."

"I can't be responsible for what my men do."

She gave him a derisive look. "You just told me you were powerful enough to do whatever you want. Now you can't control your men? I'm beginning to think you're all talk and no action."

If she wanted a reaction from him, she got it in the way his nostrils flared with fury as his eyes shot daggers at her.

"Best see to Jamie and Carrie," she told him.

"You've got until the end of the day to turn everything over to me."

That gave her precious little time to . . . what? It wasn't as if there was a plan or anything. Halfling or not, she couldn't stand against Bran and his army. Still, something told her to ask for more time.

"I need more than a handful of hours to—"

"What?" Bran interrupted. "Pack? You're leaving with the clothes you have on your back and nothing else. Not even your sister's vehicle." He smirked at her. "See you at sunset."

The silence after he departed was so loud that her ears rang with it. She closed her eyes as a wealth of emotions threatened to pull her under.

After being in Daire's arms, she'd believed that everything would work out. How could it not with a Fae such as he by her side? And then the rest of the Reapers came. They were set to win.

Daire spoke of taking precautions so Bran wouldn't know the Reapers were there. Either Daire lied, or Bran was that good. Not that it mattered now. Because the Reapers had left her all alone to deal with a madman.

She walked into the cottage and stood by the door. Her gaze wandered around the kitchen to the biscuits, scones, and cakes

Carrie had made. There was also enough breakfast food to feed an army twice over.

Ettie made her way to the stove and shut off everything. Usually, she couldn't pass up anything Carrie baked, but the delicious aromas did nothing for her now.

She walked to the cabinet and put her hand atop the ancient piece for a few moments. Then she continued on, pausing at the doorways of her sisters' bedrooms before ending up in hers.

The rumpled bed and the indent on the second pillow were reminders that Daire had stayed the night with her. Images of them making love beneath the sultry Greek moon flashed in her mind. It was all too much for her to handle.

She leaned back against the wall and slid down as tears filled her eyes. Ettie covered her face with her hands and released the flood. She cried so hard her shoulders shook, her body aching at Daire's betrayal.

Was anything he told her true? She'd felt sorry for him and how his friends deceived him. It was the one thing she figured he'd never do to her because he knew how it felt. So why had he?

There had been such honesty in his eyes when he spoke to her. She'd believed everything he said, taking him at his word. How could she have been so wrong?

"Daire!" she screamed as she raised her head.

She wanted answers. And he would give them to her.

"Daire! Show yourself, now!"

Through the tears, she looked around the room, waiting for him to show himself. But the seconds turned to minutes. That's when she knew, the Reapers weren't going to help her. They'd seen that they couldn't beat Bran, so they'd retreated to fight another day.

Leaving her to match wits and brawn with a madman out to wipe them and Death from existence.

Ettie sniffed. She dropped her head back against the wall and hugged her knees to her chest. Bran felt sure of a win. So sure, in fact, that he hadn't given her options.

Most people might think that meant they were beaten. But, then again, Ettie wasn't most people. It wasn't only her body that had been trained to fight, her mind had, as well. Because the strongest opponent could be brought down by a slower, weaker foe when they used their minds.

The fact that Bran didn't give her alternatives meant that he needed to have everything she owned. He wouldn't settle for less. But why?

He was Fae. He could get whatever vehicle, house, or land he wanted.

Unless . . . there was something else he searched for.

Ettie wiped away her tears and jumped to her feet. She only had a few hours to look through every room in the house to find what it was Bran wanted. It would be her only bargaining chip.

The universe was against him. Daire bellowed his fury as he struck the shield Bran had constructed around Ettie and the cottage with both magic and his fists.

And he wasn't the only one.

The Reapers—sans Cael—were doing the same, but not causing a dent in Bran's magic. Making the situation even worse was the smirk on Bran's face because he could see them trying to get in.

But, apparently, Ettie couldn't.

It might have been a blessing that Daire couldn't hear what Bran said to her, but Daire would've given anything to have her see him trying to get to her.

"Ettie!" he yelled again as both Carrie and Jamie were taken by Bran's men.

Fintan slammed his fist into the dome, causing it to tremble. "I really want to kill that son of a bitch."

"Ditto," Neve said from the other side of the shield.

Daire ignored them as he tried to read Bran's lips. He couldn't understand the words, but he got the gist of it—Bran had given Ettie an ultimatum.

"What the feck," Cael grumbled as he appeared.

Daire threw another blast of magic at the dome. He had to get to Ettie. He feared that she believed he had left her alone to deal with Bran. Surely, she'd know he would keep his word.

Daire paused. How could she? Ettie barely knew him. He'd dumped tons of information on her and made it so she had to trust him. And now look. Her enemy confronted her, and Daire wasn't there to help.

The unfairness of the situation reminded Daire of what had happened when he discovered that his old gang murdered his family. He'd sworn never to feel that helpless, that powerless again.

No. History wasn't going to repeat itself. He'd promised to protect Ettie, and he would. Even if it cost him his life.

"Ettie!" he roared and punched the dome again and again, adding more magic each time.

Suddenly, he was hauled away, only to be tossed flat on his back with a brutal yank. He shoved away hands and tried to get to his feet. Why couldn't anyone understand that he had to get to Ettie?

"We know!" Cael shouted, his face above his.

Daire pushed at the hands, again to no avail. He didn't care what he was fighting. Soon, he wasn't able to move at all. After several more attempts, he closed his eyes, struggling for the strength to remove whatever was holding him.

"Open your fekking eyes, Daire. Look at us," Kyran said.

Confused, Daire lifted his lids. He moved his gaze in a circle around him to see all six Reapers holding him down.

Cael blew out a breath. "We're going to get to Ettie, but we need to work as a team. That means you need to control yourself."

"Let me up," Daire demanded.

"Can you control your rage?"

Daire gave a nod.

Fintan snorted loudly as he let go and stepped away. "And you all wonder why I buried my emotions."

Cael was the last to release him. As soon as he did, Daire jumped to his feet.

He looked for Ettie. "Where is she?"

"In the house," Neve said.

Daire raked his hand through his hair and dropped his chin to his chest. "How did Bran know we were here?"

"How does he ever know?" Baylon asked sarcastically.

Talin crossed his arms over his chest. "We need to get this shield down so we can talk to Ettie and figure out what's going on."

"Our magic is doing nothing. We need Death," Fintan added.

Cael was shaking his head as Fintan spoke. "We'll have to do this without her."

Daire jerked his head to Cael. "Did you talk to her? Does she know about the black sword?"

"No." Cael then turned to the dome and tested it with his magic.

Daire wasn't going to take that simple answer. He stalked to Cael and shoved at his shoulder. "What do you mean 'no?'"

"Just that. Death wasn't there."

It was the flash of anger and something . . . more . . . in Cael's eyes that stopped Daire from saying anything else. He didn't know what had happened—or didn't happen—with Death, but Cael's fury went deep.

Cael looked from him to each of the Reapers. "Bran has hurt all of us in some way. He intends to do more by killing Death and then us. Everything you're feeling, all that you are suffering, take it. Mold it into a weapon. One that you can turn on Bran."

"But we can't harm him," Neve said.

Daire called to his sword. As soon as the weight of it filled his palm, he twisted his wrist, sending the weapon dancing around him. "Then we try harder. As one. Just as Cael said."

Swords appeared in each Reaper's hand. They stood, huddled together. Cael was the first to put the tip of his blade against the dome. Daire quickly moved beside him and put his weapon next to Cael's. The others followed suit.

Then Cael pushed his magic along the blade and into the shield. Daire and the others took the cue and repeated his steps. Almost immediately, they could feel the dome shaking. And then it cracked.

"Harder!" Cael shouted.

Daire gritted his teeth and thrust his blade and magic into the crack with the others. The shield flickered a few times and then vanished.

He wasted no time rushing into the cottage and shouting Ettie's name. When there was no answer, he grew frantic while searching each room. Then he found her in Carrie's closet, searching through boxes.

"Thank the stars," he said and leaned against the doorway. His relief was so great that he was weak with it. "Ettie, please stop. There's much we need to discuss."

He frowned when she didn't so much as look his way. Daire pushed away from the door and walked to her. As soon as his hand touched her shoulder, she jerked away.

That stung, but it was nothing compared to the contempt in her gaze when she swung her head to him.

"Ettie," he began.

"Get out," she said over him.

He shook his head. "Not until you listen to what I have to say."

"Why? Because you were here when Bran took my sisters."

"I was, actually." Daire heard the others in the hallway behind him, but this was something between him and Ettie.

She curled her lip at him as she jumped to her feet. "Really? I so appreciate the help. Especially when I called for you."

"For the past several hours, we've been trying to break down a dome Bran put up, preventing us from getting to you. That was after his magic blasted me from your side when he arrived."

Ettie crossed her arms over her chest. "That's convenient."

"It's the truth," Cael said from behind him.

Daire looked into her deep blue eyes. "I'd never betray you. Somehow, Bran knew we were here, and he took actions that would make you turn against us. He made it so we wouldn't be able to come to your aid, which in turn made it appear as if we left you on your own with him."

"He took Jamie and Carrie," she said.

He found himself reaching for her, but he dropped his arm at the last moment because he couldn't take her pulling away from him again. "We saw. We saw everything, and he could see us. But you couldn't."

"Or you could be lying about the dome. You could've watched it all, using me to see what he wanted."

"We couldn't hear him," Daire corrected her. "And if we were going to use you as bait, we would've told you."

She looked out the window. "I don't have time for this. You need to leave."

No way was Daire giving up that easily. "Bran is a liar. Whatever he promised you, he won't keep his end of the bargain."

"How did he know we were here?" Cael asked as he came into the room.

She lifted one shoulder. "How am I supposed to know?"

"Did he ask about us?" Daire inquired.

Ettie was silent for a moment. "He asked if it was Cael who promised to protect me."

"Dammit," Cael said and turned away.

Daire saw Ettie's questioning look and said, "Bran didn't know we were here. He used his magic and the shield as a safeguard. Then he mentioned us. The fact that he didn't know it was me means he didn't have a clue we were here."

"Until I confirmed his suspicions." Her face crumpled as her arms dropped to her side.

Neve said, "He does this to everyone, Ettie. Don't take it personally."

Ettie's face was lined with hope as she looked at him. "Were you really prohibited from getting to me?"

"We want Bran dead. We've no reason to lie to you," Daire told her. "Bran manipulates and lies. You can't trust him."

She licked her lips and drew in a shuddering breath. "He took my sisters so that I'd turn over the property, the cottage, and everything in it. He said I could only leave with the clothes on my back."

"Just when I didn't think I could hate the asshole more," Baylon grumbled.

Fintan grunted in reply.

Daire turned to the side to see the others as well as Ettie. "Bran wants something here."

"That's what I think, as well," Ettie said. "I've been searching the rooms to see if I could find it, but I've come up with nothing."

Cael waved his hand at her words. "It'll be magical."

"The dirt?" Ettie asked.

Daire shook his head. "There isn't enough magic in it."

"Then I don't know," she said in frustration.

Kyran grinned and winked at her. "Guess it's a good thing you've got Reapers as friends."

"Spread out over the cottage and buildings," Daire said.

Cael gave Ettie a nod. "If it's here, we'll find it."

Daire started to follow the others when Ettie's hand stopped him. He turned to her, and with only a small hesitation, she flew into his arms.

He held her tightly, his eyes closing at the feeling of her against him. "I was ready to move Heaven and Earth to get to you."

"Bran was so convincing," she murmured.

"We'll face him together next time."

She lifted her head to look at him. "He's coming here at sunset. I'm supposed to sign over everything in exchange for my sisters then."

"We'll figure something out so you don't lose your home."

"I'd rather have my sisters."

He cupped her face. "I'll do everything I can to save them."

"I didn't say that you were here, but I didn't say you weren't. Maybe if I had, Bran wouldn't have known."

"Don't," Daire told her. "I dropped my veil and attacked the dome while he was talking to you. He saw me. It doesn't matter how he found out, Bran knows now."

She drew in a deep breath. "It changes things, doesn't it?"

"It means the element of surprise we wanted is gone, but we're not giving up. So don't give up on me."

"I did."

"And you had every right to," he told her.

She shook her head, frowning. "I shouldn't have, and I'm sorry."

"We're in this together, remember? Because if we fail, then it isn't just the Fae who will feel the repercussions, Halflings and mortals will, as well."

She looked up at him apologetically. "I didn't think about that. If I had—"

He put a finger to her lips. "Stop talking and kiss me."

Her smile was slow as the worry fell from her face. She pulled his head down as she rose up on her toes and pressed her lips against his.

As their tongues dueled and the flames of desire lapped at him, Daire realized something that he prayed Bran didn't know—that he'd fallen for the warrior Halfling.

CHAPTER
seventeen

He was so close. Closer than ever. Bran could practically taste the victory. Though he'd dreamed of being the one to deliver the killing blow to Death, he'd come to terms with the fact that someone else would have to do it.

That wasn't the case any longer.

He lovingly ran a finger along the weathered page with its eloquent writing as he sat in a chair in the master bedroom. The burned edges with a piece of the lower right corner missing wordlessly spoke of how someone had attempted to get rid of the evidence.

It was the drawing on the upper left side that had caught his attention. The first time he'd read the page, he didn't realize it had been written by Death herself.

The sheet had been torn from a journal where Death poured her heart out and wrote of being the Mistress of War. Even now, the drawing of her called to him on a primal level.

Her long, black hair was pulled away from her face to fall down her back. She wore armor from her elbows to her waist that glittered with gold, silver, and black. It wasn't bulky, but thin and made just for her. It hugged her body, showing off all her feminine assets while allowing her to move freely.

A black leather skirt that hung to mid-thigh had strips of chainmail and armor falling from her waist. Gold gauntlets covered her wrists and the backs of her hands while black boots encased her lower legs up to her knees.

And in her hand was a black sword that looked as if smoke were billowing from it.

This had been Death before she turned into the serene being she was now. As laughable as that was, the page with her words and the drawing allowed him to extract her magic.

He hadn't realized it at first, but the moment Bran felt the power fill him, he'd known the cause. Every time he looked at the picture or read her writing, he got more of her magic. It was a wonderful, thrilling thing. Which was why no one else knew of the sheet—not even Searlas.

There was no way the Reapers or Death would ever figure out how he was stealing her power. Only as he stood over Erith, holding her black sword to strike his deathblow, would he tell her how her downfall came to be.

He couldn't wait until that moment. It wouldn't bring back his love, but it was the first step in his quest for vengeance. Death's rules had been pointless. He'd lost the woman he loved, as well as his own freedom, only to discover that Erith had changed the rules for her new Reapers.

They were now allowed to not only marry but also bring their women into the fold. For that, Death would watch each of her Reapers die slow, painful deaths. Cael would be last.

It was only fitting that the Fae she'd chosen as the leader of the Reapers would be helpless to stop his own death—and hers.

Bran closed his eyes, picturing it all unfolding in his mind. Then he took a deep breath and opened his eyes while he made the page vanish.

He heard a commotion downstairs and rose to his feet. Opening the door, he listened as the O'Byrne sisters yelled obscenities at his men. Bran smiled at their spunk and descended the stairs where they were being held in the library.

"Enough," he bellowed as he strode in.

The sisters turned their gazes to him. If looks could kill, he would've been charred on the spot. There was no doubt they were of his blood.

"You bastard," Jamie said between clenched teeth.

He stopped before them. His magic alone held them to their chairs, preventing them from moving. While he controlled their bodies, he hadn't done the same with their mouths.

"If you don't stop the infernal screaming, I will make it so you can't speak," he threatened.

Carrie threw him a condemning look. "Enjoy this power while you can because it won't last."

"Why?" he asked. "Because the Reapers are helping you?"

Jamie barked in laughter. "Because we're going to kill you."

"I think not."

"Let me up," Carrie said. "Try fighting me."

Bran wasn't stupid. He wasn't going to test the Halflings. Not after what had happened with Catriona. "You'll only be here a few more hours. Then, if your sister does what she's supposed to, you'll be released to her."

"That's not what you promised me," Searlas said as he fingered Carrie's long, blond hair.

"After they're returned, she's all yours," he said. "It's not as if they can stop you."

Carrie jerked her head away from Searlas while Jamie glared in Bran's direction.

"It's always difficult for anyone to realize they're prisoners," Bran stated.

Jamie asked, "What are you having Ettie do?"

"Nothing, really. She's signing over the deed to the land and house as well as everything within it to me. In return, I'll hand you to her. Then, the three of you are on your own."

Carrie tried to bite Searlas's hand when it drew too close to her mouth. "Right. That's because you told this bumbling oaf that I was his afterward. I'll be sure to mention that to Ettie."

"Oh, my dear," Bran said as he squatted down before her. "Do you really think I'll allow you to talk?"

He laughed as her face paled. Bran got to his feet and looked at the sisters. This was all almost too easy. Though it didn't hurt that he was taking a jab at the Reapers.

It infuriated him that they'd somehow managed to learn where he was and tried to interfere once more. But he'd stopped them quickly enough. It was almost laughable how effortless it was to turn someone against another.

With just a little magic in the shield and a few words to Ettie, she would never trust the Reapers again. Not that the Reapers would ever break through the dome. He'd almost hated to leave them. It had been quite entertaining to watch as they struggled to make a dent in his magic.

Maybe now they'd realize that it didn't matter how much power and magic they had, they didn't stand a chance against him.

"Ettie isn't going to give you a damn thing," Jamie said.

Bran raised a brow as he met her gaze. "Are you so sure of that? To save the two of you?"

"We have nothing," Carrie announced.

"That's where you're wrong."

Jamie frowned as she snorted. "Trust me. We don't have anything you want."

"The very land you live on, the cottage that's been handed down through generations of O'Byrnes. Why do you think it hasn't left your family since they acquired it? Generations upon generations of your ancestors have been born and died there, while the rest of the world left behind their family homes."

It irritated Bran that he'd accepted the lie Ettie told him about the land being split between the three sisters. If he hadn't done a bit of searching on his own at the county offices, he wouldn't know of her falsehood. But that had been rectified easily enough.

Carrie began laughing, softly at first, but it grew until her shoulders shook with it.

"Something amusing?" Bran inquired, irritation swirling within him. He hated being laughed at.

She nodded, her smile wide. "I'm imagining your face when Ettie signs over everything and you realize there's nothing there."

Bran glanced at the ceiling as he put his hands behind his back. Then he moved to stand between the two girls and bent at the waist so he was even with their faces. He looked from one to the other.

"If anyone is going to look the fool, it's you. I wonder if anyone in your family even knew what it was they had. I don't think they did, because if so, Ettie would never let it go. Not even to save you."

He smiled when their faces paled.

Erith lay beneath the sun as she watched the clouds move overhead. Except she didn't see them. Instead, she saw Cael's face before he'd left her realm the last time.

There had been hurt and anger in his words. She'd stepped away from the window in case he looked for her, but he hadn't so much as given the tower a glance. The image of him stalking away with clenched fists and a rigid back was seared into her mind.

It had been difficult not to go to Cael and find out what he wanted. He never came to her for trivial matters, but her decision was for the best. Besides, Cael was the leader of the Reapers because he was more than capable of figuring out things on his own. He didn't need her. He'd never needed her.

She sighed. It was bad enough that Seamus was there to see her decline when she'd much rather die alone.

That wasn't true.

No one wanted to die alone. She'd seen enough beings suffer through various kinds of deaths on their own, and it was always better with others around. Dying was something every living entity eventually did.

And that included her.

Though she hadn't expected it for many more years. Now that it was upon her, she found herself doing what all others did— looking back on her life. There was much she regretted, much more she didn't. Things she wished she could change, and some she was glad had happened as they did.

Her musings were interrupted by the sound of Seamus approaching. He came to stand beside her before he sat and looked out over the cliff to the sea below.

"You're making a mistake," he said.

She linked her fingers over her stomach. "I know you think so."

"Hurting Cael isn't the answer."

"I'm protecting him."

Seamus turned his head to look at her. "No. You're protecting yourself."

"So what if I am?"

He ruefully shook his head. "I don't care if you turn back into the Mistress of War. I'd rather you be that than no longer alive."

She sat up, never taking her gaze from his. "You wouldn't say that if you knew what I was."

"I do." With that, he tossed down a book.

Erith stared at the tome, her heart skipping a beat. She'd forgotten that was in the library. She'd tried to put her past behind her.

"I know all about you," Seamus continued. "I know the wars you caused, the devastation you left in your wake, and the lives taken. But through it all, you were still Death."

She pulled her gaze from the book to look back at Seamus. "Yes, I'm Death. I claim the Fae whose time it is to die. But it's so much more than that."

"I don't care, and neither would any of the Reapers. You formed them to fight for you. Why not fight alongside them?"

"Because if I did, they would die, too."

Seamus leaned his head to the side, his lips twisting. "You chose each of the Reapers because of their battle skills and their integrity, loyalty, and persistence. They're the best of the best. Trust them."

"It's hard to do that when I know what happens to those around me when I go into battle."

"But you'd be fighting for yourself, for everything you've built. You'd be fighting for your Reapers, the men and women who vowed to serve you. This isn't about liking war and wanting to see death. This is about delivering justice. Which is what you do."

He had a point, much as she wished he didn't. "It may be too late. I'm weak."

"I've been thinking about that." Seamus ran a hand over his mouth and along his jaw. "Let me leave. I'll make it so that Bran finds me. He'll let me get close since I helped to free him. That way, I can find out how he's stealing your magic and stop him."

"You're asking me to trust that you won't betray me."

He gave a nod of his head. "I am."

"Each of my Reapers was betrayed. It doesn't matter how minor, those treacheries are horrid, even to those who only witnessed them."

"I'm on your side. I won't betray you."

Erith looked back over the sea. She was probably too drained to be much good in a fight against Bran, even if she gave in to to the need for war within her. So, if Seamus betrayed her, it would only quicken her death.

Which might be a kindness.

"Find Cael first," she ordered. "Tell him what you're doing, and tell him I've sealed this realm so no one can enter."

"Erith, you should tell Cael everything."

She sighed. "I won't, and neither will you. I still have strength enough to strike you down, no matter if you're with Bran or not."

"I won't let you down," Seamus vowed softly.

Her head turned to him when he lifted her hand and kissed the back of it. He knew she didn't like being touched, but she allowed it. His red gaze met hers then.

"May the sun shine upon you and light your way through the darkness," she said.

With one last grin, the Dark got to his feet and departed.

Now, she was truly alone.

eighteen

Chaos could be a beautiful thing. That's exactly how Ettie saw the state of her home and the Reapers—chaos. Everyone moved in different directions in various ways, but all of it was in harmony.

Because they'd come together for a common goal.

The problem was that after hours of searching, they had nothing to show for it. Ettie blew a strand of hair out of her eyes and slapped her hands on her thighs as she sat back on her haunches after looking beneath her bed.

"Nothing. There's nothing," she grumbled.

"I wish that were true," Cael said as he walked into the room with Daire. "Bran wouldn't be so adamant if he thought for a moment whatever he looked for was somewhere else."

Daire shoved his long hair back from his face. "Cael's right."

"Well, it'd be helpful if we knew what it was." She climbed to her feet and faced them.

"Every room has been thoroughly searched," Daire said.

Cael shut a drawer of the bureau. "As has the shed. It could be buried."

"Bran mentioned the house, so I just assumed it was in here, but you could be right," Ettie replied. "It could be buried. Why then ask for the house and the land."

"In case it's hidden beneath the house," Daire replied.

She plopped down on the bed. "The object could be absolutely anything. We have thirteen acres of land. There's no way we can search all of it before sunset."

"Have you ever seen a black sword?"

Daire's question took her aback. "A black sword? Never. If that were around here, my father would've likely hung it up. Why?"

"Just curious," he said.

But it was the look Cael gave Daire that led her to believe it was much more than that. Cael slipped away, leaving them alone. It was just the opportunity she needed.

She caught Daire's gaze. "Tell me about the sword."

"It's probably nothing."

"Or it could be something."

He took her hand as he sat beside her. The contact reminded her of their lovemaking and how she craved his touch.

"This morning while you slept, I looked over to find you holding a black sword," Daire said.

"I think I would've known if something like that were in my hand."

"As soon as you woke, it disappeared."

She jumped up in surprise and fear. Her gaze went to the bed and then her hands. "That's . . . what is it?"

"I believe it's a Fae sword."

When he didn't elaborate more, she raised her brows and asked, "Annnnd?"

"Remember when I called that weapon for you? I do the same with my sword. When I no longer need it, I put it back."

"Put it where?"

"It's magic, Ettie. I can't really explain where it goes, other than to say it's my space. No one else can get to the things I have there."

A laugh bubbled up in her at the hilarity of thinking she had such a thing. "Trust me, if I had such a space, I'd tell you."

"I don't think you know about it."

"A secret magical space I don't know about." She gave a frustrated shake of her head. "So what do I do?"

He rose and came to stand before her. As she looked into his eyes, she began to relax. He placed his hands on either side of her face, gently holding her as he leaned down and kissed her.

They'd been discussing swords and secret magical places, so the kiss wasn't just unexpected, it was greatly needed. She melted against him, her arms wrapping around his middle.

Just being held by Daire changed her entire attitude. The stress that had been building eased, and the tension slowly evaporated until there was nothing but blinding, consuming desire.

The kiss deepened as a moan rumbled in his chest. His sounds made her hot and achy, but it was his hands, mouth, and body that brought her ecstasy.

He broke the kiss and gazed down at her. "It's all I can do not to throw you onto that bed and make love to you."

"That sounds like heaven."

But it wasn't time for such things. With longing in their eyes, they reluctantly set aside their hunger for each other. Once Bran was defeated, they would have all the time they wanted. At least, she hoped they would.

Daire placed his hands on her shoulders. "Close your eyes and put your hands by your sides."

She did as he asked, taking a deep breath in the process.

"The Fae are born with this ability, but some Halflings are able to do it with practice."

That wasn't exactly comforting, but she didn't tell him that. Instead, she concentrated on her breathing.

Daire moved behind her and put his mouth by her ear. "Picture a black sword in your mind."

"What size and shape? What abo—"

"It doesn't matter," he interrupted. "Concentrate. It's important. Do you have a mental picture?"

She nodded.

"Good. Now, I need you to imagine holding it in your hand. It could take several tries, but don't stop your focus."

Ettie had no problem envisioning the sword in her hand. She did it again and again, but felt nothing in her palm. After a few minutes, she glanced at her hand to find it empty.

"This is pointless," she said and turned to Daire.

There was a deep frown on his face. "It should've worked."

"Maybe you just thought you saw the sword."

"I saw it," he insisted. "You don't forget something like that."

She crossed her arms over her chest, feeling like a failure. "I'm sorry."

"This isn't your fault." He held her face between his hands and looked deep into her eyes. "If it's meant to happen, then it will. And if it doesn't, then that's fine, too."

His words did much to bolster her. She put her hands on his arms and smiled up at him. But she could tell that he'd really counted on her retrieving the sword.

What was the deal with her and Fae weapons? Why couldn't she hold one? And why had Daire seen her holding a black sword? It was all just too much.

The door to the cottage swung open as Cael strode in. The rest of the Reapers filed in behind him. She and Daire dropped their arms and walked into the living room.

"We need to prepare for Bran," Cael said.

Daire nodded, his face tight with concentration. "I've been thinking about that. He went to a lot of trouble to make Ettie believe she couldn't trust us."

"You want to use that," Kyran said.

Daire flashed a grin. "I do. We need to put the dome back into place."

Ettie jerked her head to him. "Tell me you'll be inside this time."

"Some of us will." Daire looked to the others. "Cael, Bran needs to see you outside."

Cael's hands clenched at his sides. "I'll give him a show."

"And the rest of us?" Neve asked.

Daire pointed to Cael, Baylon, Talin, and Neve. "You four remain where he can see you. I, Fintan, and Kyran will be within the dome."

"Until you find out what it is Bran wants," Ettie said as comprehension dawned.

"Exactly. Once we have that, the shield will come down, and the others will be there."

Ettie loved the idea, but she hesitated. "You said you couldn't kill him."

"But you can," Cael said.

She blinked before swinging her eyes to Daire. "It takes a Fae weapon to kill Bran. Need I remind you that I can't hold one of those? How am I supposed to kill him without one?"

"She'll be slaughtered without the proper weapons," Neve said.

Daire rubbed the back of his neck. "There has to be a way."

Ettie watched as he called forth the same spear as before. He held it out to her, and she paused before reaching for it. As soon as her fingers closed around it, the weapon vanished like before.

"Let me," Talin said.

She stood as first Talin, then Baylon, and then Fintan all tried to give her a weapon. Next was Neve and Kyran, to no avail.

Finally, Cael stood before her. His silver gaze looked her over before he held a sword out for her. "Take it," he urged. "Believe that it's yours."

She took a deep breath, letting his words sink in. The sword could end all her troubles—as well as the Reapers'. She was skilled enough to get in a killing blow. The only hang-up was that she needed a Fae weapon.

The weapon is mine. The weapon is mine. The weapon is mine.

Over and over she repeated those words to herself. Then she clasped her hand on the sword. She felt the metal of the hilt in her palm. Just as she began to lift it, the sword disappeared.

"She had it," Daire said.

Cael crossed his arms over his chest and sighed. "That she did."

"So why can't I keep it?" she asked.

Cael's lips flattened briefly. "That's a damn good question."

"We need Death," Neve said.

But Cael dismissed her words outright. "We do this on our own.

"Cael," Fintan said. "This could be what ends Bran. Death should be here to help us."

"We do this on our own!" Cael bellowed.

Ettie swallowed hard after his outburst. The looks of confusion and shock on the Reapers' faces told her that the outburst was out of the ordinary for Cael.

Talin stepped close to Cael. "What's going on?"

"Death is taking care of other business. She won't be here to help us," Cael explained.

Ettie didn't know whether to be disappointed that she wouldn't meet Death or glad. Perhaps it was the latter. After all, she was Death.

"This plan sounds solid," Ettie said. "All except for the fact that I can't harm Bran."

Daire blew out a breath. "We need to come up with a different plan then. I'm not putting you near Bran."

"You don't have a choice," she told him. "I have to meet with him to sign over my property."

Neve snorted loudly. "Which is shit, I must say."

"I agree, but what choice do I have? He has Jamie and Carrie."

"He won't turn them over to you," Fintan said.

Baylon's nose wrinkled in distaste. "Or if he does, his men will return later for them."

"He gave me his word," Ettie said, appalled at the idea of losing her sisters despite everything.

Daire met her gaze. "He can't be trusted."

"Yet he expects me to keep my word?" How she hated the situation.

Any way she looked at it, she was trapped. Because Bran had Jamie and Carrie. Ettie had no choice but to give him exactly what he wanted. And that galled her.

Daire took her hand, holding it tightly. "As soon as he releases Jamie and Carrie, we'll take all three of you away."

"That's our only option, isn't it?" she asked.

Cael twisted his lips. "Anything else will likely end in the deaths of your sisters as well as you."

The room felt heavy with frustration and anger. It was no

wonder the Reapers wanted Bran killed so badly. Every time they turned around, they were fighting him with few options available to end his spree of violence.

If only she could hold a Fae weapon, then all of it could end that night. But for whatever reason, Fae weapons were out of her reach.

She looked out the window to see the sun sinking behind the mountains. Her time was up.

For all her years of training, not once had Ettie realized how that which was spoken had more power than a weapon or fist. It was words that had changed her fate starting with her father, then Daire, and now Bran.

Except it was Bran who wanted to destroy everything she had.

Daire was attempting to help her keep what was hers.

She shivered against the cold as well as the fear that threatened to crush her. Each time she thought how differently things could've gone had Daire and the Reapers not found her, her stomach pitched.

But Daire had found her. Now, she stood a chance against Bran. It was a slim one, but it was better than what she would have had without Daire and the Reapers.

She fisted her hands in the pockets of her jacket. She was a Halfling. A human with Fae blood. It set her family apart from others. Partly because the magic of her ancestry allowed those in her family to excel at certain things.

Yet it was the attention placed upon them by the Fae that really made the difference.

Every few minutes, she tried to call the sword as Daire had shown her, but her mind wasn't focused. Any second now, Bran would arrive to demand everything she owned in exchange for her sisters.

She would have to match wits with him again, and frankly, she wasn't sure she was up for it. Though she didn't have a choice. The responsibility fell to her. Except, this time, the lives of her sisters were on the line.

Every action she took, every word that passed her lips would determine their fates. This time, she was skidding on ice, slamming against one wall or another, unable to right herself.

It was a horrible sensation. She was putting all of her faith and trust in Daire and the Reapers. If anything went wrong. . . .

No. She wouldn't think like that. She had to stay positive. For her sisters and for herself.

She faced the sunset, watching the giant orange ball dip below the mountains. The last little bit of light that vanished in a blip made her feel as if she were shrouded in darkness now, as if she were the last soul on earth.

The waiting was the hardest part. She expected Bran to arrive the minute the sun was gone, but he was nowhere to be seen. The bastard was toying with her.

Her temper flared, but she managed to keep it in check. She wanted to shout and scream his name, to call him out and demand he show himself. But she kept her mouth shut.

This wasn't just about her family. This was about all Fae, and if she were honest, all humans, as well. Bran had to be stopped. She'd seen the evil in his silver eyes. It didn't take a lot of imagining to realize what he could do if he were able to defeat Death and take that position himself.

She wasn't about to face Bran just for herself, but also for the Reapers, the Fae, Halflings, and all of humanity. Her training had consisted of using her hands and body to fight—not her wits. Yet that's exactly what she was about to do.

Whether it was because she was hyper aware or just more focused, she knew the moment Bran arrived. He stood behind her, and somehow, she managed to ignore him despite the chill that skittered down her spine at his arrival.

"Are you looking for the Reapers?" Bran asked in a mocking voice.

Ettie took a deep breath and slowly released it. "Where are Jamie and Carrie?"

"Safe."

"Nothing is happening until I see them."

Bran snapped his fingers, the sound as loud as a shot in the quiet valley. Almost at once, her sisters appeared, each held by a Dark.

Ettie's heart skipped a beat when she gazed into the blood red eyes of the Dark Fae holding Jamie. The one restraining Carrie wouldn't stop staring at her baby sister.

Daire was right. Bran wasn't going to let any of them free. As soon as he had what he wanted, his army would take her sisters away. They might take her, too, but it wouldn't surprise her if Bran made sure she was left alone never to know what had become of her family.

"There they are," Bran said. "I do believe we had an agreement."

Ettie faced him. She was suddenly calm, something that

should've frightened her, but she gladly accepted it. She would use it against Bran because she didn't know how long it would last.

"Our agreement was for you to release my sisters, unharmed, in exchange for me signing over the land, house, and our belongings to you," she said.

Bran's lips curved into a smile. "That's right."

"You hold all the cards. I have nothing to use against you."

"Again, that's correct."

His smile widened, and she controlled the urge to punch him in the face. "I can't stand against you, or any Fae."

"Your point?"

"Why didn't you demand all of this from the beginning?"

Bran chuckled and moved a step closer to her. "It was a game."

"A game? With a half-Fae? Did you need to feel superior?"

"I am superior. In every way," he stated. "It amused me to see how I could bend you to my will."

She cocked a brow. "It amused you? Are you in such need of entertainment that you find your descendants only to mess with their minds and destroy their lives?"

"What fun would it have been for me to show up and simply force you to give me what I want?"

"You've done that anyway."

The smile dropped. His face hardened with anger and a malevolence so revolting that she took a step back. "I get what I want. Always."

"What is it exactly that you want here?"

"Why should I tell you?"

She shrugged, her lips twisting. "Why not? It's not as if I can stop you."

"How can you be of my blood and unable to protect yourself?" he asked as he sneered at her.

"You're the one attacking your own kin."

He rubbed a hand over his chin. "I should warn you that trying to make me feel pity or remorse is useless. Even if you were my own daughter, I'd still do this."

"How were you ever Light?"

"What you see now is the result of Death. Everything I am now is Death's fault."

Ettie snorted. "You don't think your actions caused things?"

"Do you want to die, Ettie?"

She'd known that threat would come. "I don't, but we both know I won't be leaving here alive. Just as we both know you never had any intention of releasing my sisters."

"A spark of potential." Bran clasped his hands behind his back and grinned. "So you're not as stupid as I originally thought. Is this where you try to bargain with me?"

"No."

"Ah. Your intelligence is growing by the second. Why not?"

She gave him a flat look. "As I stated earlier, you hold all the cards. I have nothing."

He looked her over and preened. "No. You don't."

She held his gaze, refusing to look away. "I just want one thing."

"What's that? For me to allow you and your sisters to live?"

"I want to know what it is you've come for. Tell me why I'm giving up my home and my life."

"Why should I?"

She lifted one shoulder in a shrug. "Why not tell me? It's simple curiosity. Nothing more."

"Why aren't you asking for your life?"

"Would you give it to me?"

"No."

She flattened her lips. "Precisely."

"Everyone begs. Everyone."

"I'm not everyone."

His gaze narrowed on her. "You'll beg for your sisters."

She hadn't looked their way since they arrived, and Ettie wouldn't now either. She might very well break if she did. "What good will it do? You have your mind made up."

"I want to hear you beg."

"Tell me what you've come for, and I'll do it."

"I thought you said you had nothing to bargain with."

She gave a bark of laughter and shook her head. "I stood here for hours trying to think of what we could have that would cause you to go to such extremes, and I came up with nothing. I'm completely alone. You've made sure of that."

"The Reapers were never a group you could count on."

"They were all I had."

"So you gave them your trust."

She slowly nodded. "I didn't expect them to abandon me."

"They're no match for me, and they know it."

"I don't care anymore about them. I've lived my entire life preparing for an event that was never explained to me. Now, I'll never know what I was training for. The least you can do is show me what you're searching for."

He studied her for a long moment before looking over her shoulder. At his smile, she knew he must have spotted Cael and the others.

From what Ettie could see, none of Bran's men realized the Reapers were inside the dome with them. So far, at least.

"A sword."

She blinked, her stomach falling to her feet. "A sword."

"One that was discarded eons ago. It's buried here."

Ettie started shaking her head. "If something like that was here, my family would've known. We would've dug it up and protected it."

Bran laughed. "That would be rather difficult since it's far below the earth. The blade is so powerful that Fae are repelled by it. It's why there's none of my kind in Killarney."

"But you're here. As were the Reapers."

"We're different," Bran stated.

Ettie was going to be sick. She didn't need to ask what it looked like to know that it was a black blade. How had it come to be in her grip?

She pulled her hands from her pockets and dropped them to her sides. Then she imagined the weapon in her hand. But there was nothing. "You believe you can find the sword?"

"Of course."

Within her mind, she screamed "No!" The sound reverberated in her head and through her soul. She knew then that she had to protect the sword at all costs.

The weight of something suddenly filled her hand. Ettie glanced over to see the thick wooden spear with the long blade at the end that Daire had tried to give her. She turned and twirled the spear before she pointed it at Bran.

"You're not touching that sword," she stated.

Daire didn't know who was more surprised when Ettie called up a weapon, him or her. There was a brief widening of her eyes before she faced off with Bran. Daire motioned to Kyran and Fintan to spread out from their places behind the garage.

When Bran arrived, he didn't check to see if any Reapers were within the shield. That told Daire just how confident Bran was in his ability. It also meant that they would get their surprise attack.

And they needed to make the most of it.

While Daire came up behind Bran, Cael was on the outside of the dome punching the barrier while Neve, Talin, and Baylon did the same. Bran didn't pay any of them a moment's notice. Which was just what Daire wanted.

Bran slowly dropped his arms to his sides when Ettie pointed the spear at him. "Don't think I won't kill you and your sisters."

"You can try," Ettie said.

Daire didn't know how she got the spear, and he didn't care.

Not only had she called up a weapon, but it was Fae. Which meant it could kill Bran if she were able to get in a good hit.

Bran was close enough that Daire could wrap his hands around the bastard's neck. He might not be able to strike the ending blow, but he could set everything up.

Their plan had been to get the girls out. That changed the moment Ettie called up the weapon. Daire glanced at Fintan and Kyran, who stood near Searlas and the other Dark who held the sisters.

Daire called up his sword. As soon as Ettie spun and attacked, the Reapers inside the shield dropped their veils and launched themselves at the Dark.

Fintan gutted Searlas while Kyran slashed the throat of the other Dark before Fintan teleported away with Jamie and Carrie. Daire kicked the backs of Bran's knees, buckling them so he went down on all fours.

The dome vanished, and the rest of the Reapers spilled into the area. Ettie used that time to jab the spear toward Bran's heart. He leaned to the side at the last minute, causing the blade to pierce his arm.

He let out a bellow and jumped to his feet. With his lips peeled back and his teeth bared, Bran ignored Daire and went straight for Ettie.

Daire and Cael closed in on Bran while Ettie used the spear to knock away the orbs of magic Bran threw at her as he advanced. Meanwhile, more of Bran's army arrived. Soon, the valley was filled with the sounds of battle.

Despite her training, Ettie was no match for the sheer power of Bran. Daire saw her weakening and sought to turn Bran's attention to him. He let a large bubble of magic form in his hand before he hurled it at Bran's back.

Bran jerked at the impact of the orb and halted. He shifted to look Daire's way before turning back to Ettie. Except, this time, it was Cael who stood in his way.

Daire teleported to Ettie's side and moved her away from Bran. Sweat covered her face, causing her hair to stick to her cheeks and neck. He held out his hand to her. Ettie's fingers linked with his.

"It's not your time, Cael," Bran said, causing Daire to turn his focus back to the pair.

With a wave of Bran's hand, Cael was surrounded by twenty Dark, who immediately began attacking him. Daire glanced at Ettie, who gave him a nod of assurance. They dropped their hands and prepared for Bran's assault.

"You can't stop me," Bran said to Daire.

Daire tightened his grip on his sword. "We'll see about that."

As one, Daire and Ettie attacked Bran. With no weapon, Bran used his body to block them and his magic to thwart them. But Daire didn't give up. Neither did Ettie.

Again and again, they attacked. Ettie got in several strikes, but none was a killing blow. Worse, she was growing tired. She might be a Halfling, but she didn't have the stamina of a Fae, which put her at a distinct disadvantage.

Daire knew they needed to find an opening for Ettie before she was too exhausted to deliver the killing blow. He launched a vicious attack on Bran that focused all of Bran's attention on him.

His plan allowed Ettie a few seconds to catch her breath, but that's all she got before Bran hurled two large orbs of magic right at Daire. He managed to knock one aside, but the other hit his left side.

Daire pushed aside the pain. Out of the corner of his eye, he spotted Cael and Fintan fighting side by side. With Ettie's sisters away, Bran no longer had any leverage over Ettie. But that didn't mean she was safe. In fact, it meant she was in even more danger.

Ignoring the burning in his side, Daire rushed toward Ettie right as she went in for another attack on Bran. Only this time, her leg gave out. She fell to one knee before rolling on the ground and coming up on her feet.

She recovered, but not quickly enough. Bran was waiting for her, as if he'd anticipated her move. He knocked the spear out of her hands and swept her feet out from under her.

Daire's heart stopped. He shouted her name as everything moved in slow motion. Ettie was on her knees, looking up at Bran, who held a massive bubble of magic.

It didn't matter how fast Daire moved, he wouldn't make it to Ettie in time. He threw his sword at Bran in an attempt to buy her some time. The blade impaled itself in Bran's upper arm, but that didn't even draw Bran's attention.

Daire gritted his teeth and teleported to Ettie, even as Bran's hand started the downward arc toward her. Daire was about to witness her death, and no matter his outrage, he wouldn't be able to do a damn thing to Bran.

"Nooooooo!" he yelled as he slid on his knees toward Ettie to knock her out of the way and take the magic himself.

Except when she raised her hands over her head, something flickered and appeared. He gaped in astonishment when his gaze landed on the black sword.

The bubble of magic landed on the sword and ricocheted off. For a second, no one moved as they all stared at the weapon. Then Ettie gave a battle yell and swung the blade toward Bran.

Just when Daire thought the nightmare would end, Bran vanished before the blade could touch him. A second later, the rest of his army followed.

Daire watched as Ettie slowly lowered the sword. He was close enough to touch it, but it was the last thing he wanted to do. There was something about the weapon that made him want to get far, far away from it.

"Well, shit," Kyran murmured as he walked up.

One by one, the other Reapers approached, yet none of them tried to touch the sword. And then, without a word or movement, it disappeared.

"I didn't do that," Ettie said.

Cael released a breath. "It served its purpose. Now it's gone again."

"Served its purpose?" Neve asked.

Daire took Ettie's hand, and they climbed to their feet. "That sword belongs to a powerful being. Bran said it was discarded here where it's lain dormant."

"Not completely inactive," Fintan pointed out. "It protected Ettie."

Baylon cleared his throat. "Well, I for one am glad it's gone. I didn't want to be anywhere near it."

"None of us did," Talin said.

Ettie leaned against Daire. "Is it over? Is Bran gone?"

"He'll be back," Cael said. "But for now, it's over."

Daire wrapped an arm around her. "You can't remain here."

"Then who'll protect the sword?" she asked.

He looked up at Cael. "I think the sword guards itself. If it wanted to be with Bran, it would've gone to him."

"Daire's right," Cael said.

Ettie held out her hand and tried to call for the weapon. She tried for several minutes before she lowered her arm. "Now what?" she asked.

With a nod, Cael and the others teleported away. Daire turned to Ettie and smiled down at her. "The decision is yours. We'll keep your sisters safeguarded until we can end this threat with Bran."

"Where are Jamie and Carrie?"

"I don't know exactly where Fintan took them, but we need only ask him."

She licked her lips. "All right."

"You can stay here if you wish, but I wouldn't recommend it. Bran will return."

"What do you think I should do?"

"Come with me."

She glanced at the ground. "With you?"

"Yes. I want to make sure Bran can't get to you, but I also want to see more of you."

"Do you?" she asked with a grin.

He smoothed her hair back from her face. "I . . . well, I have feelings for you."

"What kinds of feelings?" she pressed.

He looked up at the stars, feeling a bit sick to his stomach. He hadn't wanted to put anything into words. Not yet, at least. They barely knew each other, but the one thing he did know above all else was that he wanted Ettie in his life.

His gaze lowered to her. "I care about you. Deeply. In fact . . . I'm pretty sure I'm falling for you."

"Pretty sure?" she asked as a blond bow arched.

"Certain. I'm certain," he amended.

She nodded and took a step closer to him, placing her hands on his chest. "So, if I told you that I'm certain I've fallen head over heels in love with you, you wouldn't freak out?"

"Freak . . . ?" His heart pounded in his chest as happiness and excitement filled him. "No, I wouldn't freak out at all."

"You sure?"

It was then that he saw the teasing light in her blue eyes. He tucked a strand of blond hair behind her ear. "Certain of it."

They shared a smile before she released a deep breath. "What will Death say?"

"I don't know. Whoever that black sword belongs to is powerful enough that you being able to wield it means something."

"I have a feeling that will only work if I'm here."

"Exactly," he said. "There's something important about this land, which means you're valuable. Even if that weren't the case, I'd fight to keep you with me."

She ran a finger along his lips. "Why?" she asked in a whisper.

"Because with you, everything makes sense. It's like I can finally understand things."

"As if the glasses have come off and you can see clearly," she offered.

"Exactly."

She smiled. "I feel the same. Complete."

"Yes."

Suddenly, she stepped out of his arms and walked into the cottage. Daire followed her inside and found her standing in front of the cabinet. She unlocked it and opened the doors before she reached inside for something. When she turned around, she was holding the jar of dirt.

"I know what this is."

He frowned and walked to her. "What?"

"It's this land. It's dirt from beneath our feet."

Daire took the jar, rolling it around as he stared at the dark earth within the glass. "The residual magic I feel is from the sword. But how did your ancestors know to take this?"

"Probably the same way I knew what the dirt was."

"The sword talks to you?"

She shook her head, her forehead crinkling. "It's more like a feeling. Like the truth has always been there, but I can see it now that I've held the sword."

"I think you'd better keep this with you," he said as he handed her the jar.

Ettie tucked it against her. "It needs to be somewhere safe."

"I know just the place." Daire held out his hand. As soon as she placed her palm against his, he teleported them to Inchmickery.

twenty-one

Safety was something she'd always taken for granted, but Ettie learned the true meaning of the word after Daire teleported her to Inchmickery.

She knew how powerful Bran was, but not even that dampened her spirit on the small isle. A fierce winter storm battered the fort. The winds howled, and the rain lashed the buildings, but Ettie didn't mind. She explored the rooms while watching the interaction between the Reapers and their women.

For the first time in days, she was able to breathe easier because she knew Bran couldn't get to her or her sisters. Jamie and Carrie were also at the fort, but they wouldn't remain much longer.

Ettie smiled when she felt Daire move up behind her before he wrapped his arms around her. She leaned back against him and covered his hands with hers.

"You don't have to watch your sisters," he said.

She looked into the room where River was reading one of her

books, and Cat was talking to Jamie. A moment later, Carrie walked in with a tray of tea and biscuits.

"I like watching," Ettie said.

Daire rested his chin atop her head. "Are you going to be all right with your sisters leaving?"

"It's time. It's been time."

"You'll be able to see them whenever you want."

She turned around in his arms and looked up at him. "I know. I'm really fine with Jamie and Carrie setting out on their own together."

"Cael found them a nice place in—"

She put her finger over his lips to stop his words. "My sisters will be safe. They'll have a life."

"Bran could come for them eventually."

She dropped her hand to his shoulder and shrugged. "I don't think so. He had his chance to get the sword, and it didn't work."

"He won't give up that easily."

"No doubt you're right, but he'll go about it another way. Now that the land is vacant, he'll search for it himself."

Daire bent and gave her a soft kiss. "But that's a worry for tomorrow."

"Is it really okay that I'm here?"

"Yes."

She raised a brow. "And Death? How does she feel?"

"She will no doubt wish to talk to you."

Ettie smiled. "Should I be worried about her visit?"

"I'm not going to lie, Death is intense. But she's also fair. Cael said she's away right now."

"Does she not want to fight Bran for her magic?"

"That's what we're doing," he said.

Ettie glanced at her sisters over her shoulder. "While Death gets weaker, Bran gets stronger. We need something that can beat him."

"I think we found it. Or, rather, you did."

"The sword," she said with a nod. "I've been wondering about that. I don't know how it appeared. I didn't even think about it."

He took her hand and led her down the corridor. "I believe it's attuned to you. It's why it appeared when you needed it most."

"And you think I can do that again?"

"It's worth a try."

"That it is. Anything to put Bran back in the Netherworld."

A muscle jumped in Daire's jaw. "I don't think he'll survive what we have planned for him."

She glanced into the room where Cael, Fintan, and Baylon were deep in conversation. Then she looked up at Daire. "Bran is a murderer. He deserves whatever is coming to him."

"And I get to do all of it with you by my side," Daire said with a grin.

"Do the girls really want me to start training them?"

He leaned against the wall and nodded. "Neve will be with the Reapers, so she can't train them. You, however, can."

"Because I'll be staying behind to guard them and this place." It was a heavy burden, but she willingly and happily took on the responsibility.

"Damn, you make me proud."

She beamed up at him. "It seems everyone is busy."

"So it does," he said with a sly grin.

There were no words needed as they hurried through the hallways to the room he'd claimed as his. They shut the door behind them as they came together, their lips meeting as the passion took them.

Ettie didn't wonder or worry what the future held. Why would she when she was in the arms of someone like Daire? He was everything to her, and the fact that she was now part of the war only completed everything she'd trained for.

This is what she was meant to do. And Daire was who she was supposed to be with.

"I love you," she said as he kissed down her throat.

His head lifted as he looked at her. "Together, we face whatever comes our way, bound by our love."

"Together." She threaded her fingers into his long, black hair and gazed into his eyes.

"Bound."

She pulled his head down for a kiss, sealing their words as effectively as if they were vows. Because they were.

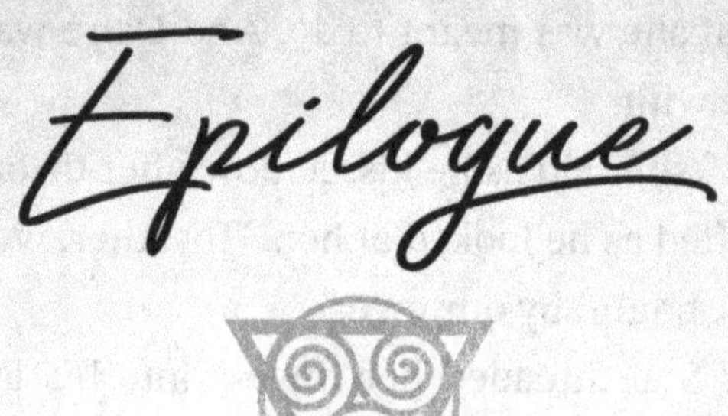

Epilogue

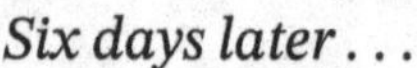

Six days later . . .

Every morning, Daire woke smiling. How could he not with Ettie by his side? Though he was beginning to worry about why Erith hadn't paid them a visit. She always did after a mission, and this one had been particularly interesting because of the black sword.

Daire left Ettie sleeping and made his way to Cael's office. He found their leader sitting on the sofa with one arm resting on the back while he stared at the opposite wall. "What aren't you telling us?"

Cael sighed and swung his head toward him. "A lot."

"About Erith."

"Even more."

"Should I be worried that she's not come to talk to Ettie?"

Cael lowered his arm and sat forward. "I don't know."

"Should we call for her?"

"It wouldn't do any good."

Daire frowned as he took a step farther into the room. He stared at Cael a long moment as realization dawned. "You've been calling for her."

"A few times, yes. She's either unable to answer, or unwilling."

"I'm not sure which is worse."

Cael ran a hand down his face. "I have a bad feeling about what's to come. We've thwarted Bran again, but these small victories are getting us nowhere."

"You think something bigger is coming."

"I feel it in my bones. We need Eoghan. We need Erith. Both are missing."

Daire felt as if he'd been sucker punched. "What do you mean Death is missing?"

"Do you have another word for her absence?"

He didn't. Daire blew out a breath. "Erith will always do her own thing. If she's not answering, I have to believe it's because she doesn't want to. As for Eoghan, he's out there."

"Then let's find him."

"What about Bran?"

Cael got to his feet. "Eoghan is our priority now."

"About damn time," Daire said with a smile, eager to begin.

Bran walked the O'Byrne land. Despite his considerable power and magic, nothing he'd done produced the black blade. For the past twelve hours, he'd tried every spell, every command he knew, to no avail.

The sword, it seemed, had a will of its own.

Ettie was with the Reapers—Daire in particular. Jamie and

Carrie were also missing, though it wouldn't take much for him to find them.

In order to deliver the final blow to Erith, he needed her blade. He'd believed it would be easy to obtain. Not once had he considered the O'Byrnes to be any sort of roadblock. Yet, that's exactly what they'd been.

But there was always more than one way to get what he wanted. As elusive as the black blade was, it would eventually be in his grasp.

"Enjoy your time, Erith," he said. "It's coming to an end."

He called up the journal page and read her words as more of her magic flowed into him.

Eoghan was huddled with his head down and his back against what felt like rock. Since he could see nothing but darkness, he wasn't exactly sure what he touched.

But even without any light, the being that hunted him could be felt. So far, Eoghan had kept just out of its reach. He didn't remember how he'd come to be on the realm, or who had bound him for the beast.

For all he knew, he could be blind.

Eoghan lifted his face, wishing to feel the sun upon his skin. There was no doubt in his mind that Cael and the others searched for him. But not even that gave him hope that they'd find him.

He didn't know how long he'd been on the realm. He should be searching for a way out, but his days were spent staying one step head of the thing that hunted him.

Eoghan stood and looked behind him. The beast's search was

bringing him closer. Eoghan hurried away, tripping over rocks. He winced when he scraped his skin, but he kept moving.

He didn't know how long he walked before he heard it. The sound was so faint at first that he almost thought it was only in his head. He kept moving towards the noise, and as he did, it grew to a soft whisper . . . music.

A violin to be exact.

The melody was haunting, evocative. Its melancholy sound moved Eoghan's very soul. An inner voice urged him to seek the source. He told himself it was to better hear the tune, but he knew there was more to it.

Like a golden thread that shimmered in the night, he followed the music.

Thank you for reading **DARK ALPHA'S NIGHT**.
I hope you enjoyed Daire and Ettie's story as much as I enjoyed writing it.

If you want more Reapers, then you're in luck!
Up next is **DARK ALPHA'S HUNGER**.

BUY DARK ALPHA'S HUNGER NOW
at www.DonnaGrant.com

◆

And don't miss out on the Dark Kings series.
The next book set in Dark Universe, is **TORCHED**...

BUY TORCHED NOW
at www.DonnaGrant.com

✦

To find out when new books release
SIGN UP FOR MY NEWSLETTER today at
https://www.tinyurl.com/DonnaGrantNews

Join my Facebook group, Donna Grant Groupies, for exclusive
giveaways and sneak peeks of future books.
https://bit.ly/DGGroupies

✦

Keep reading for a peek of DARK ALPHA'S HUNGER and a
glimpse at TORCHED ...

SNEAK PEEK AT DARK ALPHA'S HUNGER

REAPER SERIES, BOOK 6

I am a Reaper—an elite assassin bound to Death.

I follow the command. I take the mark. Nothing stops me.

Not even the darkness that finally dragged me under.

I should have been lost to it forever.

But one sound pulled me back—her music.

Thea is a Half-Fae, cautious yet fierce, and her music awakens a hunger I've never allowed myself to feel.

Every note pulls me closer.

Every breath around her tests the control I swore never to break.

Her melodies cut through the void, and pull me into the light, leading me back to my brethren...and into a rising war. Whoever hunts her may be the key to uncovering the enemy stalking us all.

For her, I'll shatter my vow of silence.

For her, I'll face the shadows still clinging to my soul.

For her...

I'll risk everything.

***New York Times* and *USA Today* bestselling author Donna Grant delivers a dark, sensual tale of danger, desire, and the love powerful enough to pull even a Reaper from the edge.**

BUY DARK ALPHA'S HUNGER TODAY
at www.DonnaGrant.com

Excerpt

Kilkenny, Ireland
February

The portal stones stood against the sunset like giants. And just like many years earlier, they called to her, urging her closer.

Thea's hand tightened on her violin case. It had been nearly three weeks since her last visit to the stones, and each time the same anxiety, the same restlessness filled her. As if her belonging there were preordained.

From the very first time she had seen the megalithic structure, she had been struck by its beauty. And its mystery.

"Leac an Scail," she whispered as she walked closer. Stone of the warrior.

Kilmogue was one of the largest dolmens in all of Ireland. Without a doubt, it was one of the most impressive. It stood twelve feet high with the capstone over thirteen feet long.

Thea reached the stones and set down her case. She rested her hand on one of the boulders and felt the warmth that seemed to radiate out from the inside.

She walked all around the dolmen, looking at the capstone resting on two large boulders with a pillow stone laying on its backstone. She stopped at the entrance that faced northeast with the enormous doorstone almost ten feet high.

For long minutes, she stood in the doorway. Once, about ten years ago, she'd almost gotten the nerve to walk inside. They weren't called portal stones for nothing. But she lacked the courage then. And now.

Instead, she visited the dolmen as often as she could, waiting to see what the stones wanted from her. Because she knew they desired something. Otherwise, why would they continue to call her back?

Thea retrieved her case and gently laid it flat to open it. Then she pulled out the violin and tucked it beneath her chin as she found the bow. She placed her fingers on the strings and closed her eyes to let the music find her. The notes constantly floated around in her mind, forming melodies and songs without any effort. Today was no different.

Placing her bow on the strings, she gently pulled it back, hearing the first soft tones. She gave herself to the music, the notes rising and falling on their own.

And her body played as if controlled by another.

Song after song fell from her hands, filling the air. She lost track of time, as she usually did while playing. But there was nothing purer or more beautiful than music.

It fed her soul as nothing else could. And it had saved her.

At only eight years of age, she had struggled to get through each day. Utterly alone and buried in depression—so low that she actually begged to die while in the children's home. It wasn't death that she was given, but a violin.

Ms. Fylan, who smiled without saying a word, had placed the instrument in Thea's hands. For weeks, Thea sat in music class without attempting to play. Each day, she found herself looking forward to hearing more of the tunes.

Nearly two months passed before she tried to play the violin. From her first cringe-worthy note, she discovered her passion.

While Ms. Fylan had given her the instrument, ultimately, it was the music that saved Thea.

She'd never found a foster family. Instead, she spent her days in the children's home until she was able to go out into the world. Those formative years made her strong enough to survive on her own.

She worked numerous jobs to pay for University. It didn't matter how long her day was or how exhausted she felt, she never went to bed without playing her violin.

That's how Duane found her. He'd been walking home from a gig at a nearby tavern and heard her through an open window. He'd called up to her. While Thea never thought to play in a band, Duane's offer intrigued her.

The next day, she went for an audition, and two nights later, she was performing her first gig. It paid so well that it became her sole source of income.

Returning from her reverie, she finished the last song and let the note fade away. Thea opened her eyes as she lowered her bow arm. Darkness surrounded her, with nothing but the moonlight and stars to light the way.

The inside of the portal stones was black as pitch, but for just a moment, she thought she heard something within. It had been a deep rumbling, almost like a . . . growl.

Thea swallowed, her heart beginning to pound against her chest. She contemplated leaving, but the pull of the stones was too strong.

With the sounds of the night all around her—and nothing coming from the dolmen—she adjusted her chin and began to play again.

Except she kept her eyes open this time. So many times, she'd come to play, but nothing like this had ever happened before. It was a little frightening. Then again, it would take much more than some sound to make her run away.

The way her mood had turned, Thea wasn't surprised when the music shifted from something soft and soothing to a somber, stirring song.

She swayed with the gripping melody. Each note slid through her body until she felt it in every muscle, every bone. She was so engrossed in the music that, at first, she didn't see the glow emanating from within the portal stones.

Thea stepped back and tried to stop playing but she couldn't. The music continued, almost of its own accord. Her gaze was locked on the doorway as the soft pinpoint of light grew larger in diameter.

The edges of the radiance rippled as if it were water. She gasped, her heart jumping into her throat when a hand appeared out of the light.

With fingers spread wide, the appendage reached for something, anything to grab hold of. As more of the arm appeared, she saw the veins protruding and muscles flexing. Almost as if it were taking every bit of strength for whoever was coming through just to pull themselves out.

Suddenly, the arm was yanked back into the darkness until only the wrist and hand remained. Thea set her violin in its case and hesitantly started toward the doorway. She had to turn her head to the side and shield her eyes because the light was so bright.

"What the bloody hell are you doing?" she asked herself.

No one in their right mind would walk toward the scary light and hand. Then again, what kind of sane person played a violin in front of some portal stones?

Thea hesitated another moment before she reached out and grasped the hand. Strong fingers wrapped around hers. The grip was tight and bordered on painful, but she didn't let go. Not even when she was pulled toward the light.

She dug her heels into the earth and used both hands to yank on the appendage. Thea gritted her teeth and used all of her strength to drag the person out —and stop herself from being pulled in.

More of the arm appeared. A moment later, the shoulder. Then a second arm latched onto Thea. That was the only warning she had before she saw the muscles flex in the limbs as the hands yanked.

The heels of her boots sank deeper into the dirt and left trails as she was dragged forward. Somehow, she knew that whoever this was wasn't trying to pull her in. They were attempting to get out. Since there was nothing else for the person to grab onto, she was acting like a rope.

Her eyes widened when a head appeared. Long, inky black hair hung all around the face. Then the chin lifted, and liquid silver eyes speared her.

She found herself staring at a man—a very gorgeous, dirty man.

His face was lined with determination. Suddenly, he looked back into the light and bared his teeth as he growled. But it was the answering rumble of something dark and nefarious that caused her heart to skip a beat.

The man said nothing as he returned his gaze to her. She renewed her efforts while he continued to pull himself out. Finally, he got one leg free and set his foot on the ground. She glanced down and saw that his jeans were in tatters, his limbs coated in blood.

He threw back his head and howled in pain and anger. Thea thought she saw something dark begin to emerge behind him. She barely caught sight of it before the man roughly shoved her away.

It was so unexpected that she stumbled back, trying to get her legs beneath her. Instead, she slammed against one of the portal rocks, knocking the back of her head as she did. Pain exploded, causing her to black out for a second.

She heard grunts but could see little of the fighting because of the bright light. She struggled to get the pain under control so she could see. When she was finally able to focus again, she saw the man hitting what appeared to be a black blob.

Then, he turned and grabbed her. He lifted her in one arm as if she were a sack. Then he tossed her out of the dolmen. She landed hard on her side and rolled. When she stopped, she looked up to find him standing before the portal stones with his legs spread as if he were ready for . . . something.

He had his back to her so she couldn't see his face, but she did glimpse what looked like an iridescent orb that continued to grow bigger and bigger in his hand. Then he threw it at the light.

There was a second of silence before the dolmen exploded. Thea ducked her face and covered her head with her arms. She felt the man land heavily on top of her to shield her from the debris that rained down upon them.

It felt like forever before he rolled off onto his back. Thea glanced at him before she rose up on her elbows to look at him. His quicksilver eyes were locked on her.

She gaped at them and the fact that there were no pupils to be seen. Only pools of beautiful of what looked like liquid mercury.

"Run," he whispered before his eyes closed.

BUY DARK ALPHA'S HUNGER NOW
at www.DonnaGrant.com

GLIMPSE AT THE NEXT DARK UNIVERSE BOOK

TORCHED, DARK KINGS SERIES, BOOK 13

The King of Silvers. Cunning, perceptive, resourceful. Determined. Banished from Dreagan eons ago because of a betrayal that shattered his entire existence, his sole focus in life is to exact revenge against the Dragon Kings. A formidable fighter with centuries of rage on his side, Ulrik will stop at nothing to take down those who exiled him.

He has been alone, trusting no one for thousands of years. Until she walks into his life. He should not yearn for her, but there is no stopping the fiercely burning attraction. When he's with her, he isn't thinking of war or revenge. He only thinks about her, craves her. Burns for her. But soon he will be forced to choose: Will he continue on his course of destruction, or will he be able to set aside his vengeance to save the woman who risked everything for him.

BUY TORCHED TODAY
at www.DonnaGrant.com

ABOUT THE AUTHOR

New York Times and *USA Today* bestselling author Donna Grant® has been praised for her "totally addictive" and "unique and sensual" stories.

She's written more than one hundred novels spanning multiple genres of romance including the bestselling Dragon Kings® series that features a thrilling combination of Druids, Fae, and immortal Highlanders who are dark, dangerous, and irresistible. She lives in Texas with her dog and a cat.

www.DonnaGrant.com

www.MotherofDragonsBooks.com

facebook.com/AuthorDonnaGrant

instagram.com/dgauthor

tiktok.com/@donnagrant_author

bookbub.com/authors/donna-grant

goodreads.com/donna_grant

pinterest.com/donnagrant1

www.ingramcontent.com/pod-product-compliance
Lightning Source LLC
Chambersburg PA
CBHW011152190726
48288CB00010B/3277